"I think it's time to go back to the doctor."

There was a long silence on the other end of the phone. Then her mom said slowly, "You feel bad, Sarah?"

"Yes."

They both knew that Sarah didn't panic easily. Her mother's voice didn't waver, but Sarah knew the effort it must have taken. "Okay, I'll call the doctor's office. Try not to worry. You've beaten it before, Sweetheart. You can do it again."

"Sure," Sarah murmured, but she had to bite her lip as she hung up the phone. She'd had two remissions already. How many miracles was anyone allowed?

Dear Diary
Family Secrets

Don't miss the next book in this touching series

DEAR DIARY
BLUE MOON
by Susan E. Kirby

*Coming in August 1996
from Berkley Books*

The *Dear Diary* Series

FAMILY SECRETS

Cheryl Zach

BERKLEY BOOKS, NEW YORK

FAMILY SECRETS

A Berkley Book / published by arrangement with the author

PRINTING HISTORY
Berkley edition / May 1996

ISBN: 0-425-15292-8

BERKLEY®
Berkley Books are published by The Berkley Publishing Group,
200 Madison Avenue, New York, New York 10016.
BERKLEY and the "B" design
are trademarks belonging to Berkley Publishing Corporation.

PRINTED IN THE UNITED STATES OF AMERICA

10 9 8 7 6 5 4 3 2

This book is dedicated to
the Leukemia Society of America,
and to everyone who works to cure cancer and to
help those who live with its challenges.

Chapter
One

Dear Diary,

It's back, I know it's back. I can feel it when I wake up in the morning, that dragging tiredness that never quite goes away no matter how long I sleep.

It's so unfair. In a few weeks I'll start my senior year of high school. All my friends will be with me, and now there's Mark. Yesterday he asked me out again—this is the third time. I think he really likes me. I have the senior prom to look forward to, and the senior trip, and colleges to visit. My English teacher says I'm sure to get a scholarship. I wanted it to be a great year.

I wasn't planning to die.

Sarah Davenport closed her diary and looked out her bedroom window into California sunshine. Past the apartment buildings and across the busy avenue lined by tall palm trees, dozens of sailboats were lined up along the marina; they shifted slightly in the water as she watched. Their tall masts, with sails furled, stood as erect as a forest of leafless trees. One boat moved serenely down the channel toward open water, its white sails flashing in the golden sunlight.

She could smell the tang of the salty breeze through the open window and hear, over the screech of tires, the noisy call of sea gulls. The air was warm and balmy. It was a beautiful day for living. The irony made her throat close up, and her vision blurred for a moment.

She blinked hard; she detested self-pity. But she barely heard the knock on the apartment door as she struggled for composure.

The knocking came again, and a call from behind the door. "Sarah Lee, are you in there?"

Sarah grinned unwillingly. Her best friend Maria, whom she'd known forever, knew how much she hated the dessert label nickname. One boyfriend, of remarkably short duration, had called her "Cupcake" and "Creampuff" till she had dumped a cream-topped fudge cake into his lap. It had ended their brief relationship, but she'd had no regrets. He'd been too stuck on himself anyhow, she remembered now, nothing like Mark.

"I'm coming," she shouted. Trying to ignore the fatigue that pulled at her limbs, she headed for the door, flipping the lock and letting in her old friend.

"Hey, why aren't you in your bathing suit? I

thought we were walking down to the beach," Maria said in surprise.

"I don't feel—I'm not in the mood today," Sarah murmured, not quite meeting her friend's eye.

"Why the long face? You and Mark have a fight?"

Sarah shook her head. The silence was telling, and when Maria spoke again, her tone was more sober. "It's not time for a checkup, is it?"

Maria knew how nervous Sarah got before her usual six-month tests. Sarah sighed. "No, but I think it's time to go back to the doctor."

"Oh, Sarah." Maria had seen her through the last two battles, watched her unable to eat, nauseated and ill, seen her when her auburn hair had fallen out from the chemotherapy. "You think the cancer is back?"

The Big C, the dreaded word that shadowed her brightest days. Had her leukemia come back? The tests would show the results soon, but in her heart Sarah knew the answer already. She was silent, and Maria shook her head, her dark thick hair brushing her cheeks. There had been times in the past when Sarah had hated Maria for her thick, healthy hair, even while she loved her and blessed her loyalty.

"Ho-kay. I didn't really want to go to the beach. Too warm."

"Liar," Sarah argued without heat. Maria's olive skin tanned beautifully, and she had a new two-piece suit that with her well-shaped figure would draw boys like ants to a fallen ice cream cone.

"No, I mean it. You want to play a game or watch some videos?"

Sarah had to swallow. "I'm okay. I can walk down to the beach, if you want. I'll lie on a towel and watch you; I won't go into the water. No point in sitting around here." There'd be enough days when she wouldn't feel like going out, she thought glumly. She knew the routine too well. "Let me call my mom, first."

Maria nodded. "I brought some sandwiches." She glanced toward her carryall. "Got any Cokes in the fridge?"

"Sure." Sarah waved her friend toward the small neat kitchen at the other end of the apartment and picked up the phone. She'd tried her mom already earlier in the day, but had only gotten her voice mail, and this message was too cruel to trust to an answering machine.

This time she got through. "Hi, Sweetie. Everything okay?" Her mom's voice was so normal, so unsuspecting, as if sure that all the traumas were behind them. Sarah hesitated, maybe she should wait. But she'd told herself that for the last three days. It was time.

"I think I need to make an appointment with Dr. Chavas," she said very carefully, willing herself not to allow her voice to thicken.

There was a long silence on the other end of the

phone. Then her mom said slowly, "You feel bad, Sarah?"

"Yes."

They both knew that Sarah didn't panic easily. Her mother's voice didn't waver, but Sarah knew the effort it must have taken. "Okay, I'll call the doctor's office. Try not to worry. You've beaten it before, Sweetheart. You can do it again."

"Sure," Sarah murmured, but she had to bite her lip as she hung up the phone. She'd had two remissions already. How many miracles was anyone allowed?

Chapter
Two

Dear Diary,

I have my first chemo session today. It makes me sick to my stomach just to think about it. I hate it all—the strong medicine smells, the needles, being attached to the IV for hours at a time. It makes me feel trapped, like a dog chained to a post—I never could stand to see a dog on a chain. I feel so helpless.

Sarah put her diary away and looked at the clock. As if on cue, her mother came into the room, car keys in her hand.

"Are you ready, Sarah?"

She wanted to shout, "No, I'm not ready. I don't want to do this all again—I hate it all; I hate having cancer, I hate being sick." Some of her thoughts must have been reflected in her face, because her mother frowned.

"Dumb question, right? No one's ever ready for this." Her mom could often pick up her thoughts

—they'd always been close, from the time Sarah had come home in Margaret Davenport's arms, wrapped in a yellow blanket, with her dad beaming at them both. Sarah didn't remember her entrance into the family, but she'd heard the story often enough.

That was another sadness, on top of many. Her dad had been here during her last bout with the disease, ready to squeeze her hand or tell a joke to try to make her laugh, even when her stomach was heaving. There was an emptiness in her life since his heart attack two years ago. But she and her mother had become even closer. What would she have done without her mom there, ready to listen anytime Sarah was lonely or confused, ready to smile at the funny things that happened at school, ready to sympathize when her first boyfriend dumped her?

Her mom always understood; they had something special between them, and Sarah never forgot to be thankful for that. Not that they didn't argue sometimes, but just normal disagreements, nothing like the continual parent-child feuding some of her friends endured.

"Sarah?"

"I'm coming." She grabbed a sweater and a book and followed her mom out of the apartment. In the parking lot she could hear the sharp cry of the sea gulls and the occasional blare of a horn from the busy street. Above them, a jet plane angled sharply upward against the blue sky and wispy clouds. LAX, Los Angeles International Airport, wasn't far away, and Sarah had grown up watching the big planes lifting off to faraway places.

Her mother unlocked their little Ford, and Sarah opened the passenger door, slipped in, and fastened her seat belt. But her thoughts were still with the plane—she'd taken only one plane ride in her lifetime, and she'd been too young to remember it. Today, she wished she were on that plane, going somewhere exciting for an exotic holiday, not in the car on her way to the hospital. Her mother maneuvered expertly through traffic, merging on the freeway into a thicker stream of cars, and Sarah shut her eyes. They'd be there soon enough.

When they parked in the hospital parking lot, Sarah saw that little had changed. Red flowers bloomed along the walk instead of orange and yellow, but the smooth white stone building was just as she remembered. They went the same way up to the oncology ward. Sarah tried not to breathe in the sharp antiseptic smells of the hospital. Her stomach was already turning.

She tried to concentrate on the relaxation techniques the cancer support group leader had taught her. Smell roses, she told her mind sternly, smell Mom's perfume. Take a deep breath and let the tension out. Think about sitting on the beach and watching the waves roll in, with Mark beside you.

The knots in her stomach eased, and Sarah was able to step off the elevator and walk down the hall, but she was still glad to reach for her mother's hand. It made her look like a little kid, maybe, but that didn't matter right now.

Her mother gripped her hand in answer, and Sarah felt better. She wasn't alone.

They checked in at the nurses' station, and Sarah saw a familiar face behind the white counter.

"Hello, Sarah," the blond woman in the pale pink uniform said, smiling.

Sarah searched her memory; Jan, it was Jan something—she sneaked a quick look at the name tag on the uniform. Yes, Jan Sullivan. She and another nurse, Alice, who wore her black hair in corn rows, had been Sarah's favorites last time she'd been through chemo.

"Hi," she said, trying to smile in return.

The nurse hesitated. What did you say? Sarah wondered. "Glad to see you again" was hardly appropriate. As much as she'd appreciated the oncology nurses' kind and cheerful manner, she'd hoped never to see them in this setting again.

But instead Jan said gently, "I was so sorry to hear about your dad."

Caught off guard, Sarah had to blink hard. She missed her father so much, and especially today. Her mother squeezed her hand again, and Sarah was able to speak. "Thanks," she murmured.

Then they were directed to a treatment room, and Sarah took her seat in a long, contoured chair that allowed her to lean back and nap a little when the medicine made her drowsy.

She willed herself to relax, not to tense up, when the nurse rubbed the top of her hand with alcohol. The needle stab was slight—Jan was good with IVs. Soon the IV needle was in, taped securely so that it wouldn't pull out when she moved her hand, and connected to the hosing that led up to the bag of chemotherapy hanging on the metal pole beside the chair.

"Are you going to have the permanent catheter put back into your chest, Sarah?" the nurse asked.

Sarah shrugged. She'd had one before, but she'd had it removed—a minor surgical procedure—when her leukemia had gone into remission. While it made it easier to administer the medicine and any IV transfusions, the device also had to be cleaned and flushed every day, and it reminded her too much of the disease she'd hoped would never return. "Maybe," she murmured. "I'll see what the doctor says."

Jan nodded. "I'll be back to check on you," she said. "If you need anything, just ring."

"Want a Coke?" her mom asked. "Some crackers or fruit?"

"Not now," Sarah said. "Maybe later."

She'd brought a book to read, and she saw several magazines on the table, including a popular teen magazine—a quiet reminder that she wasn't the only young person to be fighting a serious disease.

Sarah wanted to ignore the slow drip, drip of the medicine as it slipped into her veins. Think of it fighting the cancer, she told herself; she'd discussed visualization with her support group. Think of the medicine zapping the bad cells, think about winning this battle, one more time.

She glanced at her mom, who had settled into the visitor's chair and was looking through her purse. It was harder without her dad to support them both; besides, what if Sarah didn't win, what if she died, how alone her mother would be. The thought added guilt to the layer of fear that always lurked in the back of her mind. Please, let the medicine work, she prayed now. She shut her eyes for a moment, trying not to show her anxiety.

"Sarah, are you asleep?" her mom asked softly.

Sarah opened her eyes. "Not yet." They both knew that the antinausea portion of her treatment usually made her sleepy. Sarah didn't mind sleeping through most of the treatment; it made the time go faster.

Her mother took an envelope from her purse. "This came today."

Sarah took it with her free hand. Careful not to dislodge the IV needle in her other hand, she tore open the envelope. Inside was a cheery card. "Thinking of you," the cover said, with bright flowers around the edges, and inside, she found a note in her grandmother's handwriting. "You're still the champ, Sarah. Keep your chin up. I'll call you tomorrow and we'll fight the blahs together. Much love, Nana."

Sarah blinked, then grinned. Her paternal grandmother lived north of Santa Barbara, and despite a little arthritis, she was still an active lady, and an important part of their family.

"That's nice," she told her mother, showing her the card. "When are we going to see her?"

"We'll go up on Labor Day weekend," her mother said. "I have a three-day weekend. Or she'll come down, depending."

Depending on how Sarah was feeling. Would she be better by then, or still weak from the chemo? It was impossible to say, because every time her reaction could be different. Worse, what if the medicine didn't work at all? Sarah refused to consider that possibility.

She picked up a magazine and glanced through the glossy pages, but fall fashions seemed unimportant when your life hung in the balance. And as for new hairstyles—Sarah flipped past those pages quickly. She'd probably lose her hair again, if the chemo continued long enough. She had an auburn wig in the back of her closet, but it was hot and uncomfortable. It always felt so fake that when she wore it, she just knew everyone must be staring at her head.

She tossed the magazine back on the table and opened her book instead. She was reading *Wuthering Heights,* because it was on the recommended reading list for World Lit, her senior English class.

And she was going to be there, in class with her friends, Sarah told herself now, not stuck in a hospital bed wasting away from a terminal disease. She would win out over her cancer, again.

Sarah opened the book and tried to forget the hospital room around her, tried to lose herself on an English moor with Catherine and Heathcliff. She read almost a chapter until her eyelids drooped.

When she opened her eyes again, the chair where her mother had been sitting was empty. She must have gone to the cafeteria, or to the rest room, or simply for a brief walk. The first bag of medicine had been removed, and a second (or third? How long had she slept?) hung on the IV pole. This bag had a reddish tinge, like blood. Sarah shuddered, feeling like a vampire, then with an effort, looked away.

Her mouth was dry; someone had placed a glass of water on the wide wooden arm of her chair. Sarah took a sip, and it eased the cottony feel in her throat. When her mom came back, she'd ask for a Coke. She could press the buzzer for the nurse, but the nurses worked so hard, she hated to bother them for something small. She could wait a few minutes.

When the light knock sounded, Sarah turned her head. The nurses didn't knock, nor would her mom. Maria had had a dentist appointment, but she might have gotten out early; she sometimes came by to help Sarah pass the time during a treatment. Expecting Maria, Sarah called, "Come in."

The door opened, and to her surprise Sarah saw not the tanned, smiling face of her best friend, but a tall boy with blond hair and deep blue eyes. He regarded her gravely, glancing from the startled expression on her face to the IV pole and its tubing, the taped needle on her hand, the treatment chair.

Sarah flushed, feeling the blood rush to her face, turning even her neck and chest, beneath her light cotton T-shirt, a bright red.

"Mark!"

He came in and sat down on the chair beside her. Why didn't he say something? Sarah felt awkward and acutely embarrassed.

His voice was deep, like smooth velvet. She'd never winced at the sound of it before.

"Why didn't you tell me?"

She looked away from his clear blue eyes, the same eyes she had thought about for weeks before he finally asked her out. She felt guilt at the accusing tone of his voice, but also a flicker of resentment.

"Because sometimes people treat me differently when they know. The last time I was sick, some of my friends would get tongue-tied around me, as if they didn't know what to say. I don't want to be 'the girl with cancer.' I'm still Sarah, still me, and I wanted you to think of me that way."

"I think I know you well enough to see you, and

not your disease," Mark answered, his voice steady.

She hoped it was true. "How did you find out?" she asked. "How did you know where to find me?"

"Maria," he said briefly, then added at Sarah's look of surprise, "Don't blame her; she didn't want to tell."

"I made her promise not to," Sarah murmured.

"But when you broke our date for tonight and wouldn't give me a good reason why, I thought—" This time it was his time to color slightly, and he looked away from her gaze. "I thought maybe you were going out with someone else. I called Maria and asked if you wanted to break up; I wanted to know the truth. And she said no, but I wasn't convinced, so finally she explained everything. You should have told me, Sarah."

He sounded so sure that some of Sarah's tension eased. "I'm sorry," she agreed. "I should have told you myself." And the deeper fear, that he might not want to put up with the inconvenience, the anxiety of having a girlfriend seriously ill, faded into the background. She wouldn't tell him, ever, that she'd doubted him that much.

He reached inside his windbreaker and pulled out a small stuffed animal. It was a golden lion, like their school mascot, with smooth plush skin and gleaming button eyes.

"I was going to give you this tonight. School starts soon, and I thought you could take it to the pep rallies. But I want you to have it now for a different reason. Think of him rooting for you, instead of the team."

She smiled and had to blink hard. Mark reached for her free hand, and his touch was even more comforting than the little toy. Maybe he would be up to sharing her ordeal, after all.

"Just promise you won't keep any more secrets from me," he said. "I want to know what's happening, okay?"

She nodded. "In that case, there's one more thing not everyone knows about me," she said carefully. "Maria knows, but not all my friends."

"What?"

She took a deep breath. "I'm adopted."

Mark's eyes widened in momentary surprise. "But you look a lot like your mom; you both have red hair, and you both laugh a lot."

Sarah grinned. "We even have the same laugh, Maria says, but maybe that's just because I grew up hearing her, and because we were always happy, until the cancer appeared, and then later when my dad died suddenly. As for the red hair, my mom had brown hair until I came home from the second grade in tears. We were working on family trees in class. I told the teacher I was adopted, and some of the other kids made fun of me."

"Brats," Mark murmured.

She flashed him a quick smile, but the memory still hurt a little. "They said I didn't have a real family. I didn't look like my mom and dad, I was a carrot top, and nobody really wanted me. . . . When I told my mom, she went out and had her hair tinted as close to the color of my hair as she could get it, and it's been that way ever since. That's how much she wanted me to feel that I belonged. And now she says she'd have to cover the gray with something." Sarah grinned.

Mark smiled. "You both look good as redheads," he said. "I like your mom. Do you ever wonder about your birth mother, who she was, what she was like?"

Sarah frowned. "Not much. I don't know anything about her, or my birth father, except the state they were from. If anything bothers me, it's that it's like a blank spot in a picture, a big piece of my past that's missing. Sometimes on my birthday, I wonder if she's thinking about me, if she cares how I'm doing. And I wonder why she gave me up. But I figure she did it for my benefit, and mostly, I don't think about it at all. I have a family, I have— had—two parents who loved me so much, I didn't need anything more."

Mark looked away, and for an instant her anxiety returned. Would he think she was strange, different, because she was adopted?

But his thoughts had gone another direction. "As long as we're sharing family secrets," he murmured, "you remember that I told you my parents divorced several years ago, and that I visit my dad in the summers?"

She nodded, not sure why his expression had twisted.

"It's not true," he said flatly. "I go see an uncle and aunt—my mom's brother—but I haven't seen my dad in four years. It's hard to understand how he could just walk off and leave me like that. For a long time, I tried to think what was wrong with me that he didn't want me."

He glanced at her quickly, as if not sure how she would react, but Sarah was thinking of his pain now, not her own. "Oh, Mark, that's a lousy thing for him to do."

He took a deep breath. "My stepdad's a good guy, and he takes me fishing and to the ball games, all the usual stuff. I care about him a lot, and Mom is happy, and we have a family again. But maybe you and I have more in common than you suspected."

"Could be." Sarah smiled at him despite the slight dizziness the medicine was evoking.

Maybe Mark could understand, bear up to the double burden of her secrets. Not like her first boyfriend, who'd walked away from her last bout with cancer, leaving her hurt and confused. Maybe Mark would have the courage to stay.

Chapter
Three

Dear Diary,

I've had three sessions of chemotherapy. I'm still tired, and often nauseous from the medicine, and it's a struggle just to get out of bed in the morning. School starts this week, and I want to go; I want to enjoy my senior year.

I know the treatment takes time, but I'm afraid the chemo isn't working. Dr. Chavas asked to see me this morning; I'm afraid of what she's going to say.

Sarah sat stiffly in the chair, too tense to relax against the padded cushions. The doctor's office was comfortable and pleasant, with flower prints hanging on the wall and family photos on the broad desk. Only the pile of folders and the usual wall of medical books revealed the purpose of the office, that and the omnipresent antiseptic smell that permeated any medical facility.

"How are you feeling, Sarah?" Dr. Chavas

leaned back and smiled at her. The oncologist was a dark-haired woman of Hispanic origins, and her dark brown eyes usually held a spark of hope. How the doctor could remain positive and encouraging when she had to work with patients who were often very ill, Sarah couldn't imagine.

"Lousy," Sarah told her. "Tired, no energy."

"How's the nausea?"

"Not too bad, more a queasy feeling than anything else," Sarah said. "Tell me about the results of the blood tests, please." She knew her tone sounded abrupt, but she was too nervous to wait any longer.

Her mother usually sat beside her, but today Sarah had asked her mom to wait outside. She wanted to hear the results by herself; she was all too sure she knew what the numbers would show, and she had to brace herself first, before dealing with her mother's anxiety.

The doctor's smile faded; she looked down at the folder in front of her. "I'm afraid the numbers are not what we had hoped."

She spread the papers out for Sarah to glance over; she had always been open and honest about the progress of Sarah's disease. Knowing that she knew the score helped Sarah to feel that she and the doctor and nurses were working together— part of a team; she wasn't just a pawn on a chessboard, being pushed here and there by other hands.

Sarah frowned. She didn't understand all the

test results, but she'd seen too many such reports not to realize the gist of it. "The chemo's not working, is it?"

The doctor lifted her brows. "We're not giving up, Sarah. We have another combination of drugs we can try."

"But if none of it works, what then? Is there anything else we can do?"

The doctor met her gaze. "We've discussed bone marrow transplants before, Sarah."

Sarah nodded, feeling a sinking feeling in her stomach. The bone marrow was the part inside the bone where the blood cells were made. Transplant procedure meant killing off the patient's diseased marrow and then replacing it surgically with healthy bone marrow from a donor. The process wasn't a sure cure, but it often worked, and it could cure the cancer permanently. But finding the right donor—that was the tricky part.

"As you know, the most likely candidate would be a blood relative," the doctor went on.

Sarah felt her spirits drop even more. And where were her blood relatives when she needed them? This was one thing the most loving adoptive parent couldn't provide. Her parents had both been tested the last time she'd fought the leukemia, just in case, and neither had been compatible. Finding a suitable donor who wasn't a relative was like searching for the proverbial needle in the haystack.

Sarah felt a stirring of anger toward her unknown birth mother. I need you now, Sarah thought. Where are you? Who are you? How can I find you?

She left the doctor's office feeling as if she carried a great weight on her shoulders. One last possible weapon to use against her deadly disease, and with no knowledge of her birth parents, she would come up empty-handed.

Her mother stood up as she came out into the hall. "Sarah? What did the tests show?"

Sarah struggled to speak, but she was afraid she would burst into tears. Her mom must have read the answer, and Sarah's discouragement, in her face.

Margaret Davenport took a deep breath as if to steady herself, then put an arm gently around her daughter's shoulders. "It could still turn around, Sarah."

Sarah leaned into her mother's embrace, too weary to pretend an optimism she didn't believe. "I'm tired," she said. "Let's go home."

Sarah was silent on the drive home, even shaking her head when her mother offered to stop at Sarah's favorite frozen yogurt shop.

"I'm not hungry," she murmured. The chemo treatments left a bitter taste in her mouth, and today's news hadn't helped. A bone marrow transplant—it would be expensive, if it could be done at all. Fortunately, her mom's health insurance at the bank would cover most of it. And Sarah knew her parents had been saving every penny since she first became ill, for just such an emergency. But finding the donor—that was the hardest part; it all came back to that.

When they reached the apartment, she only wanted to go to her room and lie down. But her mother touched her arm, holding her back.

"I want to show you something," she said.

Too weary to argue, Sarah followed her mother into the corner of her bedroom that she used as a study. They paused at the small desk with the computer that Margaret Davenport sometimes used for work she brought home from the office. Sarah used it, too, to type school assignments. But it was something else that her mom pulled up on the screen.

It was a letter. "What is it?" Sarah asked, only vaguely curious.

"I've been trying to find your birth mother, Sarah. I've already called Human Services in Nashville, and they said they would do what they could. The law is being changed, but right now, adoption records in Tennessee are closed, as they are in many states."

Tennessee, where she had been born, seventeen years and four months ago, Sarah thought, her curiosity stirring despite the apathy born of her ill health and low spirits. The state where her birth parents might still live. Was there any way to find them?

Answering her thought, her mother nodded toward the computer. "I've also tried several organizations that match up adopted children and birth parents, but they're strictly voluntary, and so far, neither of your birth parents has registered. So I went to the library and found a list of newspapers in Tennessee—"

She brought the list up on the computer screen, and Sarah blinked at the length of it, the number of names and addresses; it was a long list. "I've been sending letters to all of them," her mother went on. "Asking for anyone who might have information to contact us. I haven't had any responses yet, but I'm over halfway down the list. Something might come up. We might find her yet, Sarah."

Sarah knew who "her" was. Her missing, mysterious birth mother—the woman she had occasionally wondered about, despite her easy words to Mark. Who was she, and why had she given up her baby? Wouldn't she care, right now, if she knew that Sarah was fighting for her life, that Sarah needed her help to live? Sarah swallowed hard.

"Why didn't you tell me before?" she whispered, touched by her mother's determination.

"I didn't want to build up your hopes too soon," Margaret told her gently. "But we're not giving up, Sweetheart. We'll find a way."

If her mother could do so much, the least she could do was fight the depression that paralyzed her. Sarah smiled with more determination. "We will," she agreed. "And I'm starting school, tomorrow, on time."

Until that moment, she hadn't been sure she had the energy. But her mother's search gave her something new to hope for. She wasn't down for the count, not yet.

Her mom smiled. "Why don't you rest for a while? I'll make some soup for dinner."

Sarah nodded. As she went into her bedroom, the phone rang. Maria or Mark, she guessed. Sitting down on the bed, she picked up her little stuffed lion as she reached for the phone. She smiled when she heard Mark's voice.

"Sarah?"

"It's me," she agreed, lying back against the pile of pillows on her bed.

"How do you feel? Was it bad?"

"I didn't have chemo today," she told him. "I just went in to talk to the doctor and find out my test results."

"And?"

Sarah swallowed; she couldn't find the words. She was silent for too long.

He spoke slowly, "Not good?"

"Not good."

This time he was silent, and Sarah felt the old fear return. Would Mark find her illness, with its uncertainty, its continual ups and downs, too hard to live with? Wouldn't he rather have a healthy girlfriend, one who didn't cause him anxiety, who felt well enough to spend all day at the beach and then dance half the night?

"There's got to be something they can do," he said suddenly and forcibly.

With a sigh of relief, Sarah told him about the idea of the bone marrow transplant. "But finding a donor is very difficult," she finished. "And without blood relatives to test, the odds are against me."

"Then we'll have to do what we can to change the odds," he said firmly.

Before Sarah could ask him to explain, he went on, "Do you feel well enough to come to school tomorrow?"

"Yes," she said. "The first day of my senior year —I'm not going to miss that. We'll check out our teachers, and there'll be a special assembly, and all the club booths will be up. I'll be there."

"Good," he said. "I'll pick you up at seven-thirty."

They talked awhile longer, then Sarah hung up the phone. She wouldn't let the cancer cheat her out of her senior year—she wanted to enjoy all the activities and spend time with her friends. She would be there, please God, just as she had promised Mark, not trapped in a hospital. She pushed the dark image away; she wasn't ready to face that thought. She wasn't ready to give up.

She lay in bed until her mom called her to eat soup and hot fresh bread, with fruit afterward. Sarah ate as much as she could—nothing was as good as her mom's homemade vegetable soup— then looked into her closet and picked out an outfit to wear, loose-fitting pants that wouldn't show that she'd already lost some weight.

At least so far, she still had her hair. It looked dull and limp from the effects of the medicine, but she had a whole bathroom cabinet full of mousses and gels—she'd think of some way to make it look good. She didn't want to seem pathetic; she didn't want people to pity the "cancer victim." Sarah didn't feel like a victim—she was fighting this disease.

For a moment she wondered how many people at school were aware of her condition. Mark and Maria and the rest of her friends, and some of the teachers knew, but surely most of the kids wouldn't have heard. Sarah decided that she'd rather the whole school didn't know, didn't stare and wonder, checking her every day to see how pale she was, how weak.

"Don't be silly," she told her image in the mirror. "Who cares? I'm no movie star or president's daughter—thank goodness—just another senior."

Feeling very tired, but with a more tranquil mind, Sarah went to bed early and fell asleep right away.

At breakfast the next morning her mom offered to drive her to school.

"That's okay, Mark's picking me up," Sarah told her, trying to swallow a few bites of fruit and yogurt. Whether from her illness or just first-day jitters, her stomach was queasy, and she found it hard to eat.

"If you get too tired—" her mom said, then stopped. "You can always call me at work."

Sarah nodded, trying to make her smile optimistic. "I'll be fine," she said, and hoped it was true. "Got to go; he'll be here any minute."

She went back to her bedroom to pick up her new notebooks and took one last look in the mirror. Her hair was slicked back in a trendy style, and she picked up her makeup brush and added more blush to her cheeks, trying to add color to her too pale complexion.

The doorbell rang, and she dropped the brush. "Coming," she called, and hurried to answer the door.

Mark grinned at her and reached for her armload of notebooks, but she shook her head.

"I'm okay." She would not be treated as an invalid, not as long as she could help it.

"Have a good day," her mom called. She shrugged her suit jacket on and picked up her briefcase. "Call me if you need me."

Sarah smiled in answer and headed for Mark's car, a small red sedan with a sun roof. The air was warm; she pushed up the sun roof and enjoyed the morning sunshine on her shoulders, the salty smell of the fresh air. Rush-hour traffic clogged the avenue, and they moved slowly, giving Mark the chance to glance at her and wink.

"What is it?" she asked. His eyes were dancing

with suppressed excitement. Sarah wondered what she was missing.

"You'll see; we have a surprise for you."

Sarah wrinkled her nose, wondering what he was up to. "Good or bad?"

"Good, I hope." He turned at the intersection, then in another block pulled into the school lot and parked the car.

"Sarah!" someone called from the other side of the lot.

Sarah waved. It was Carla and Annette, two friends from the flag corps.

"You weren't at summer camp—aren't you going out for flags again?" Carla was a tall girl with short dark hair; Annette was a petite blonde. "We missed you."

Sarah shrugged. "I had to drop out for a while."

"But there's a new band director this year who's really sharp, and—"

"We'd better go in," Sarah interrupted. She hated to begin the day with explanations, to tell them that she'd been undergoing chemo sessions while they were marching on a sunny field. She'd enjoyed being part of the flag corps last year; that was another pleasure the cancer had cost her.

Inside, the bustle and noise of a hallway filled with students engulfed them and made conversation difficult. Sarah had to shout at Mark, and he yelled back, "I have to go work a booth; see you later."

Which club booth was he supporting? She tried

to remember which clubs Mark belonged to, then shook her head. And where was Maria? She wasn't at their usual meeting place.

"Come on, let's check out the club booths," Carla suggested.

Sarah had been thinking it would be nice to sit down—the fatigue never left her—but she pushed the thought aside. "Right," she agreed.

It was a school tradition that the first hour of the first day of the semester was devoted to club and booster booths; there would be exhibits and sign-ups before the regular academic day began. Sarah followed the other two girls to the gym and through the maze of exhibits and card tables that covered the padded hardwood floor.

From chess to science, gymnastics to environmental protection—the variety of displays was wide. Sarah paused to watch a chess game in progress, then tasted a bit of cheese and cracker from the French Club's exhibit. But it was a table at the very end that stopped her cold and left her heart pounding.

Red and white helium balloons floated high at the end of their strings, which were attached to the sides of the table. The large posterboard sign said SAVE A LIFE; BE TESTED AS A BONE MARROW DONOR. A large picture of Sarah, with her tall flags from one of last year's ball games, stood in the middle of the table. Mark and Maria sat behind the table, both grinning at Sarah.

So much for her anonymity. For an instant Sarah

stood very still, her cheeks flushed, and anger bubbling inside her. Now the whole school would know, and all the students would shake their heads in pity. She took a deep breath.

Mark looked so proud of his efforts, and Maria was blushing a little. They were trying to save her life, Sarah told herself. They had only meant to help. Her anger faded as quickly as it had come.

"Do you like it?" Maria asked, her tone a little anxious. "It was Mark's idea, but I thought of the balloons—red and white for blood cells, see?"

Sarah nodded. She looked at Mark, and his expression became more serious.

"We're going to do everything we can to find you a donor," he told her. "You're going to beat this, Sarah."

Sarah smiled, and the tension in her shoulders eased. He cared about her; he wasn't going to walk away. Compared to that, what did it matter how many people knew she was sick? Mark would stand by her, and Maria, and her other friends.

Carla and Annette had come up behind her. "This is for you? Why didn't you tell us, Sarah? Are you sick again?"

She nodded, but she still looked at Mark; his blue eyes were confident. Carla bent to sign her name to the list of students to be tested, and Mark winked at Sarah.

"We're going to do this, together."

Chapter
Four

Dear Diary,

The new combination of chemotherapy drugs isn't working any better than the last one. I feel more tired every day, and I had a nosebleed at school yesterday—it was so embarrassing. I got blood all over my best cotton sweater, and the whole class stared at me like I was some kind of freak.

I wanted to—no, I didn't want to die. I don't want to die; I want to live. But if we can't find a bone marrow donor who is compatible, how am I going to have any chance at all?

It wasn't that Mark and Maria and her other friends hadn't tried, Sarah thought as she put away her diary and picked up her schoolbooks.

Yesterday Mark had announced, "We've got almost five hundred people signed up, Sarah, with students and faculty and family members and anyone else we've been able to talk to."

He sounded pleased, and Sarah tried to look en-
thused. But she also had spoken to her doctor
again, and knew that so far, no suitable donors had
been found, at least not for her. Maybe someone
else would be luckier, Sarah thought; the donors
would be listed in a national bank, and somewhere, some other man or woman or child might
get that life-giving call. She hoped so, but she also
wanted some hope for herself.

"We're still signing up people," Mark added.
"Don't get discouraged, Sarah."

She tried to smile at him. But she could sense
the time running out, like one of those old hour-
glasses full of sand that she'd seen in a museum.
She could almost see her pile of sand diminishing,
slipping away into a void and never coming back.
The thought made her desperate. With so much to
worry about, it was hard to concentrate on school-
work. She'd almost flunked a trig test last week,
and usually her grades kept her at the top of the
class.

But how could she remember sines and cosines
when it was the numbers from her blood tests that
ran round and round in her head?

"You all right, Sweetheart?" her mother asked
at the breakfast table. She paused to pull a
withered leaf from one of the African violets that
sat beside the wide kitchen window, then carried a
plate of warm toast to the table.

Sarah nodded, not quite meeting her mother's
eye. They had to play at normalcy; she had to keep

pretending, yet nothing was all right, and they both knew it. It made her feel strange, this constant awareness of how little things didn't matter at all, and yet mattered a lot. "Don't complain about the cold hamburgers," she'd wanted to tell Maria in the lunchroom yesterday; "be glad you can eat." "Don't worry that your hair is frizzing with the early morning dampness," she could have told Annette when she recombed her hair in the rest room before class; "be thankful it's not falling out."

But she'd said nothing, as usual; she couldn't yell at them just because her friends were healthy and she wasn't. Besides, she'd heard more than enough talk about her cancer, about her physical condition and her state of mind. The doctor, her mother, her teachers—everyone looked at her anxiously. Sometimes Sarah just wanted to forget the whole thing, pretend she was healthy, pretend her life was okay. If she pretended hard enough, maybe it would be.

Sarah walked down to meet Mark for the ride to school, touching her own auburn hair. It had thinned a little, and it looked scraggly and limp. But so far, she hadn't gone bald, not like last time.

"Hi, how are you?" Mark leaned over to push the door open for her, and she slid into the car.

"Not bad," she said. "I think I'm going to cut my hair short—what do you think?"

"I think you'll be beautiful with hair of any length," he told her, "or with no hair at all." He winked cheerfully at her, and this time she could smile back.

Something eased inside her. It was ridiculous to worry about your hair, or lack of it, when your life was at stake, but you did, at least a little, Sarah had found.

The lift in her spirits took her through two classes, but in chemistry class the instructor announced that they would be doing experiments. Sarah joined the others as they formed a half circle around the teacher, Mr. Henry, and tried to concentrate on his instructions. But the sharp smells of the chemicals turned her too sensitive stomach. She felt a wave of nausea. Oh, great, just what she needed.

Sarah slipped out of the crowd and headed for one of the stools at the back of the room; the rest of the class crowded around the instructor. But though she perched on the tall stool, her head still whirled; she leaned back against a shelf full of supplies. She could hear the teacher's words like a bee droning in the back of her mind—the sound seemed farther and farther away. She felt the room darken, then heard someone shout; then there was the clatter of breaking glass.

"Be careful, the beakers have broken," someone was saying. "Lift her gently and move her away, but watch out for the shattered glass."

Then she opened her eyes and found she was lying on the floor, half supported by another student, while the chemistry teacher held her wrist.

"Pulse still beating," he told her calmly. "A few scratches, but nothing lethal. How do you feel?"

"Stupid," Sarah murmured, flushing at the curious glances of the other students. "I've never fainted before."

He didn't make the obvious comment. "Do you feel like standing?"

She nodded, then found that the movement made her dizzy. "I think so."

With the instructor supporting her, she got to her feet, wavering only a little.

"Everyone else sit down," Mr. Henry told his class. "John, you take her other arm. Let's walk slowly down to the nurse's office."

Sarah bit her lip; she felt so silly. But she was too weak and woozy to walk alone, and a few drops of blood oozed from a scratch on her forearm; her arm stung where the broken glass had cut her. Sarah wanted to cry from sheer exasperation and embarrassment, but she tried to hold back the tears. Not until the lab door had shut behind them did one errant tear slip out. To her relief, the chemistry teacher pretended not to see. John, the classmate who supported her on the other side, looked away. Probably he didn't know what to say, how to react. For his sake, Sarah tried to smile and blinked hard against any more tears.

When they reached the nurse's office, there was a cot for her to lie on. John and Mr. Henry returned to class, and the nurse, a middle-aged woman with soft blue eyes, cleaned the cuts from the broken glass and took her blood pressure.

Sarah shut her eyes for a moment, feeling the pressure of the cuff against her upper arm. There was a hiss as the pressure was released.

"A little low." The nurse wrote down the numbers, then looked at Sarah thoughtfully. "You might think about requesting a visiting teacher, Sarah, if coming to school gets too difficult for you."

"I don't want to stay home!" Sarah's voice sounded sharp; she wanted to yell, but knew it wouldn't help. The cancer was winning—it was taking more and more of her life away, a piece at a time. She didn't want to be stuck at home, cut off from her friends, from all the activities at school. She hated it, hated it all. The tears were back, and this time she was too weak to control them. She felt the drops slip down her cheeks and shut her eyes again.

"I'll call your mother," the school nurse said. "You just lie there and rest."

Her mother said the same thing when they got home. "Just rest awhile, Sweetheart; you look very tired."

Sarah lay across her bed, too discouraged to even pull back the sheets. She was tired of resting, tired of giving in. Why couldn't she do more to fight this thing? She didn't feel like part of the team any longer, she had no part to play.

Mark called as soon as he got home from

school. "You okay? I couldn't find you after school, and Maria told me you went home early." He sounded worried.

"We were doing experiments in chemistry class," she explained. "The smells made me sick to my stomach." She hated to tell him about fainting; she still felt embarrassed when she remembered all the watching faces. "Nothing serious."

"We signed up ten more people today to be tested as bone marrow donors," he told her. "We're over the five hundred mark, now!"

But she couldn't share his excitement. It could take five thousand, or five million, to find a bone marrow match among strangers. She needed her birth family; she needed blood relatives to test.

After she hung up the phone, Sarah rolled over and hugged her little stuffed lion. For the first time in her life, she needed her first family, the unknown parents who had given her up. Where were they?

Next morning Sarah slept late. When she opened her eyes and stared at the clock, she felt a jolt of alarm. She had missed her first class!

Then she remembered the discussion the night before, and her mom insisting she stay home for at least one day.

Sarah sighed and rolled over in bed. When she was younger, getting a day off from school would have been an unexpected treat. But now it was admitting defeat, and she hated it.

She reached for the phone on her bedside table and called her mother's office.

"How do you feel?" her mom asked.

Sarah got so tired of that question. An old first grade joke popped into her head. "With my fingers," she said.

There was silence at the other end of the phone. Was her mom mad?

"I'm glad you can joke," Margaret Davenport said. "Have you eaten?"

"I'll go down and get some yogurt from the fridge," Sarah promised.

"Call me if you need anything," her mother said. "Mrs. Wong next door said she'd look in on you at lunchtime. Call her if you need someone quickly, okay?"

Sarah hung up the phone, then walked across to open her blinds. The sky was blue, touched with high wispy clouds, and a sea gull wheeled over the marina. The air was clear enough for her to see the foothills in the distance, and a plane climbing upward from its takeoff at the airport.

Sarah sighed and went to take a container of strawberry-flavored yogurt out of the refrigerator. She took a spoon from the drawer, then came back to sit on her bed and dip the spoon into the creamy mixture while she read a chapter in her government text.

At least she could keep up with her studies. She would be back at school soon, she told herself. She didn't want to fall behind the rest of her class.

At lunchtime, Mrs. Wong came by for a few minutes, then her mother called to check on her. When Sarah put down the receiver, the phone rang again. This time it was Mark.

"I miss you," he told her.

Sarah smiled with pleasure. "I'm glad," she said. "How was the trig test?"

"Murder," Mark told her. "And we had a mugging in the school parking lot. You're missing all the excitement."

She laughed, as she knew he'd wanted, but her grin was twisted. "I hate being stuck at home," she told him. "I'll be back to school soon."

"Sure you will," he agreed quickly, but something in his tone didn't ring true.

After he hung up, Sarah stared at the phone. She had to believe she'd be back; she had to believe there was hope.

"Please, God," Sarah said aloud. "Help me to win this battle, win the war. I want to grow up, marry and have a family, have an interesting job, travel to places I've never seen. I have a whole list of things I wanted to do, a whole life I wanted to live. I'm not ready to die, not yet."

She was tired, but too restless to nap. Sarah went into her mom's room and turned on the computer. Margaret Davenport was still sending letters to the Tennessee newspaper. It wasn't very specific, the letter she'd composed. "I'm looking for information about a baby that was adopted from a young unwed mother in Tennessee seventeen years ago," it began.

"One of my friends told me to beware of cranks," her mom had explained. "I didn't want to give out too much personal information, just in case."

And they'd had one reply, but it was about a baby boy, so they still had no leads.

Sarah decided she would write her own letter; maybe hearing it from her would touch someone where her mother's more impersonal message had failed.

"I'm seventeen years old," she typed into the computer screen. "I have leukemia, and I need a bone marrow transplant from a suitable donor, most likely a blood relative. But I was adopted, and I don't know who my birth mother is or where she might be today. The transplant is my last chance, and time is running out. I want to live. If you know anything about a baby girl who was adopted from your area, please write to the following box number . . ."

She printed out ten letters and ten envelopes, folded the sheets, and inserted them into the addressed, stamped envelopes, then added them to her mother's pile.

Then she went back to her room and lay down to rest. Mark called again after school, and then Maria, and then Annette. Her mom came home with her favorite pasta salad from the Italian deli near work, and after dinner they were watching a tape together when the phone rang.

Her mom picked up the receiver. "Yes, this is she."

Her face paled, and Sarah felt her pulse quicken. "What is it?" she asked quickly.

Her mother covered the mouthpiece with one hand. "Your grandmother—she's had a heart attack."

Sarah took a deep breath, feeling tears prickle behind her eyelids. A heart attack had taken her father's life with almost no warning. Was she losing another loved one, in the midst of her own battle for life and health?

What next?

Chapter Five

Dear Diary,

I'm so worried about Nana. Mom drove up to the hospital in Santa Barbara right away, but she wouldn't let me go. Mom said she didn't know how long she'd have to stay, and she didn't want me to overtire myself. Our neighbor Mrs. Wong is "baby-sitting" me, which is embarrassing. I hate being treated like an invalid!

But at least Nana is still alive. My dad died right away; Nana's attack is not as serious; they got to her quickly, and Mom says the doctors give her a fifty-fifty chance.

Please let her live!

"Are you sure you feel okay, Sarah? I won't be at the market long," Mrs. Wong asked. Her friendly round face was creased with an unnatural frown line. Usually, her smile was the first thing you remembered about the pleasant, middle-aged widow who lived next door to them. Sarah had known her for years, and it was kind of their neighbor to move into their apartment while her mom was in Santa Barbara. Sarah just wished her health was fine, and her mom hadn't felt it necessary to have someone with her night and day.

"Sure, take your time," Sarah answered. "Here, take some of the money Mom left me to buy our groceries."

Mrs. Wong shook her head. "You might need it; I'll settle up with your mother later."

"It's okay; I also have the credit card she got for me last year, just in case of any emergency, when she had that business trip to New York," Sarah tried to explain.

But Mrs. Wong was firm. In a moment Sarah heard the apartment door shut. She closed her diary and reached for a textbook.

But Sarah was too distracted to be able to study; she sat at the kitchen table for half an hour and tried to go over her trig, but finally pushed the book away.

She'd been unable to sleep last night, and then when she finally fell into a restless slumber, she hadn't opened her eyes again until past ten. She'd wanted to call Mark, but he was already at school. She'd have to wait till the afternoon.

To her delight, Mark called from school at lunchtime. "How are you? These chicken burritos don't taste the same without you sitting beside me. I sure miss you."

"Me, too," Sarah assured him. She told him quickly about her grandmother.

Mark answered slowly, "What a rotten thing to happen. How's she doing?"

Sarah sighed. "Mom called last night, said Nana has a fighting chance. I wish I could have gone, but Mom's been spending all her time at the hospital, and she didn't want me to get overtired. But I feel awful, not going to see her myself."

Mark's reply made her sit up straighter. "I could drive you up to Santa Barbara after school. There's a band meeting, but I'm sure I can talk my way out of it. I could have you back home tonight. If it's okay with your mom, I mean."

Sarah thought quickly. "I'll tell her, but I'm sure it will be," she said. "Oh, Mark, you don't mind? That's a two-hour drive each way."

"Course not," he said. "Glad my car's running and not in the shop again. Look, I'll be there by three-thirty."

"Great." Sarah hung up the phone, feeling much better. She called the Santa Barbara hospital. Her mom wasn't in the Coronary Care waiting room, but Sarah left a message with the hospital switchboard operator.

Within ten minutes the phone rang. Sarah picked it up quickly and heard her mom's voice, sounding a little breathless.

"Sarah, is anything wrong?"

"No, no," Sarah said, angry at herself for not realizing what her mother's reaction to her message would be. "I'm fine. But I wanted to tell you that Mark says he'll drive me up after school. I can come up and see Nana, then come back home."

A silence, then her mother said slowly, "All right, if you think it won't be too much for you."

"Don't treat me like I should be wrapped in tissue paper!" Sarah snapped. Then she wanted to kick herself. Her mother had enough on her mind, between her daughter's illness and her mother-in-law's heart attack. "I'm sorry, Mom, honest. It's just—"

"I understand, Sarah. But it's hard not to be overprotective when your child is ill."

"I know." Sarah was overcome with guilt, now. "But Mark will do the driving; all I have to do is sit back and relax. I really want to see Nana."

"All right, Sweetheart. You two be careful on the freeway; drive safely."

"Right. Can I bring you anything?"

Her mother considered, then asked for more clean clothes, in case her stay at the hospital should be prolonged. Sarah wrote down the list on a notepad, happy to have something to do. She was so tired of everyone else taking charge; she wanted to do more to help her mom, her grandmother, to help herself. She was tired of being on the sidelines.

After she hung up, Sarah went into her mom's bedroom and located the clothes her mom had wanted, putting them into a hanging bag and laying it out so she wouldn't forget it when Mark arrived. A pair of sandals and some underwear went into the outside zipped pocket.

She told Mrs. Wong about the new plans when her neighbor returned, her arms full of grocery bags.

"You sure it's okay? Your mom said?" Mrs. Wong put milk and eggs and fresh fruit into the refrigerator, and packets of noodles and pasta into the cupboard.

"Absolutely, I just spoke to her." Sarah tried hard to be patient.

Mrs. Wong smiled. "That's nice, then. How about I make you some corn cloud soup for lunch?"

"That would be great," Sarah told her. "It's one of my favorites."

"Oh, I checked your mom's post office box, too," their neighbor said.

Sarah took the small assortment of mail and stuck it in her purse. She'd give it all to her mom when they reached the hospital.

After lunch, Sarah forced herself to lie down for a while; she didn't want to look tired when she reached Santa Barbara and stir up her mom's worries all over again. She got up about two and showered and blew her hair dry; it was thinner, definitely, and it looked limp. She was glad she'd had it cut shorter—maybe the sparseness wouldn't be as obvious.

She put some blush on her cheeks so she wouldn't look too pale, and was sitting on the couch, impatient to leave, when Mark rang the doorbell. She hurried to let him in.

"I got here as soon as I could," he told her, leaning to kiss her swiftly. "Ready?"

She nodded, enjoying the quick kiss. "Would you get the hang bag on the door? It's for my mom."

Mark picked up the bag and they headed for the car.

Mark told her the school news, and she leaned back against the beige upholstery, enjoying his presence. Not until a traffic slowdown made Mark give his attention to the bumper-to-bumper Los Angeles area traffic did Sarah glance down at the mail in her purse.

A department store ad, a political circular— Sarah tossed them in the backseat to save for her mom. But there was one small envelope whose handwriting she didn't recognize. And the post-mark said PLEASANT HILLS, TN. Tennessee! Was this an answer to one of their many newspaper letters?

Her heart pounded suddenly, and she found it hard to take a breath. Her mother wouldn't mind her opening it, Sarah thought; it was about Sarah, after all. She ripped the envelope open and pulled out the single sheet of lined paper. The note was alarmingly short. She was almost afraid to read it.

Sarah took a breath, then tried to focus on the small, cramped handwriting.

*I read your letter in the paper. I don't know if
this is the same baby, but I know of a baby girl
who was born on May 1 that year and adopted
shortly after, by a couple who took her back to
California. You can write to me, if you want. If
your life depends on it, I hope you find your
birth mother.*

Sarah found she was shaking. Mary Anne
Barnes, the signature said, and the return address
was on the envelope. Pleasant Hills, Tennessee.
She had never heard of the place.

Mark glanced over at her. "Sarah, are you sick?"

"No." She had to swallow hard before she could
answer. "But we have an answer to our letters, and
this time—maybe it's the right one!"

"Are you sure?" Mark's brows lifted. A truck
braked ahead of them, and he had to look back at
the crowded freeway. A jangle of too loud rap music pounded their car from the vehicle in the next
lane, and a van behind them honked impatiently.

It all sounded beautiful to Sarah's ears; she had
new hope suddenly, just when she needed it the
most. "I can't be sure, but this baby girl was born
on May 1; that's my birthday, Mark. How many
baby girls could have been adopted that year who
were born in Tennessee on that particular day?"

"I don't know; there could have been more than
one," he told her. "I guess the odds are against it."

"And she knows the baby was taken to California to live," Sarah went on.

"But the address would have told her you live in California," Mark pointed out.

"Why would she want to lie about it, get my hopes up for nothing?" Sarah argued.

"Who knows? Maybe she has a boring life and wants to be part of someone else's drama," he said.

"And maybe not. Don't you want me to find a bone marrow donor?" Sarah demanded.

He glanced at her, and she felt guilty again. How many hours had he put into the donor search, for her sake?

"That was stupid, and I didn't mean it," she told him. It seemed as if all she did was apologize. But the urgency of her need, the fear of dying—it made her irritable and left her self-control fragile. "I keep flying off the handle lately; I'm sorry, Mark."

"I know." His answer was quiet. "I hope this is the right lead, Sarah. I really do."

He put out his right hand, and she touched it, feeling the reassurance of his strong grip.

A car nosed its way into their lane, almost clipping the bumper of Mark's car, and Mark had to hit his brakes. He pulled his hand back to the steering wheel. He touched the horn, and Sarah blinked at the blare.

But she refused to give up her excitement. Surely this was the one—the correct answer to the puzzle they'd been trying to solve. Maybe the needle had been found.

For the rest of the drive, she waited impatiently to share the good news with her mother. While Mark looked for a parking place in the big hospital parking garage, Sarah got out at the entrance and hurried on into the hospital.

This time, she hardly noticed the usual hospital smells. A pleasant woman behind the information desk directed her to the second floor and the Coronary Care Unit. Sarah pressed the elevator button and hugged her purse, with the precious letter inside, under her arm.

She hurried down the hall, following the signs, and saw her mom right away inside the glass doors of the waiting area. But that first glimpse made Sarah pause outside, instead of rushing through the double doors.

Her mother looked terrible. Her face was pale, and dark shadows under her eyes made her look ten years older. Had she had any sleep at all last night? The double burden of anxiety she was carrying took on new meaning to Sarah, who felt a stab of fear for her mom's sake. What would all this stress do to Margaret Davenport's health?

She couldn't lose her mom, too—somehow, that was even worse than her fears for her own life. Her dad was dead, her grandmother gravely ill—what was the point in living if all her family had been taken away?

Sarah took a deep breath, then pushed the door open and walked through slowly. Her mom looked up.

"Sarah," she said, standing to give her daughter a hug. "Hello, Sweetheart. Where's Mark?"

"Parking the car," Sarah explained. "I was too impatient to wait. How's Nana? And how are you; you look exhausted."

"Nana's still holding her own; they said they'll know within forty-eight hours," her mother told her. "And I'm tired, but I'll be okay. You can only see her for five minutes every hour; I'll let you go in the next time."

Sarah nodded. "Have you had dinner?"

Her mother bit her lip. "No, I haven't. The cafeteria isn't exactly gourmet fare, but it's okay. Would you like to go downstairs and get something to eat?"

Sarah nodded; this time she wanted to be sure her mom ate something nourishing. She felt as if their positions were temporarily reversed. And the letter that she had been so anxious to share with her mom—that would have to wait, Sarah told herself. At least until this crisis with her grandmother was past—she wouldn't add any more stress to her mother's burden, not right now. As she looked around the waiting area, neutral in beige and cream, her next thought didn't help.

Did all this bring back the night they had rushed her dad to the emergency room? Sarah had almost blocked those terrible memories out of her mind, but this heart unit made it hard not to remember. She looked at her mother's shadowed face and felt an even deeper sympathy for her. Without words to convey what she felt, Sarah hugged her mom again.

They waited for Mark to come upstairs, then left word with the nurse at the desk and rode the elevators back down to the basement and the hospital cafeteria.

Sarah chose the salad bar, and Mark ordered a hamburger. Her mother had soup and salad. Sarah watched just as carefully as her mom had scrutinized her own meals for months, trying to be sure her mother was able to eat enough.

Mark ate quietly, and to Sarah's relief, he didn't mention the letter.

When they went back upstairs and her mother stopped at the ladies' rest room, Sarah explained quickly before following her mom inside. "I'm not going to tell her now; she's got enough to think about."

Mark nodded.

In a few minutes they all sat down again in the waiting area. When the nurse came to the door and announced the next visiting period, Sarah stood up, her mouth dry and her knees wobbly.

Inside the special care unit, she found quiet alcoves with beds surrounded by high-tech machinery. Her grandmother was in the second bed. A familiar IV hung beside her, and there were wires stuck to rubber pads on her chest that monitored her heart activity. She looked white and still, with an oxygen tube tucked into her nose, and so frail that the sight brought back all Sarah's worst fears.

But when Sarah reached out to touch the thin hand lightly, with its papery skin and swollen veins, her grandmother's eyelids lifted. Sarah smiled tremulously.

"Hi, Nana. It's me, Sarah."

"So I see." Her grandmother's voice was weaker than usual, but she sounded so much like herself that Sarah felt a little better. "How are you doing, Sassy Sarah?"

Sarah grinned. "Not too bad," she said. "I'm more worried about you, at the moment."

Her grandmother made a face, then sniffed a little at the unaccustomed annoyance of the oxygen tube inside her nostrils. "I'm a tough old bird, Sarah. I'm not turning in my library card, not just yet. What about you? Any luck with a bone marrow donor?"

Her grandmother had been tested long ago, along with most of her friends in Santa Barbara, even though her own health might have precluded her from the list of possible donors, but there had been no match.

Sarah told her about the donor drive at school, then hesitated, thinking of the letter in her purse.

"What else? I know there's something you're not telling me. We don't have long, Sarah. They have very bossy nurses in this place."

Her grandmother's wry tone made Sarah grin. "I got a letter—it may be a link to my birth parents," she almost whispered.

Her grandmother's blue eyes widened. "Wonderful! Have you called to check it out? What does Margaret say?"

"I haven't told her yet, Nana. With all this, I was afraid she had too much on her mind. When you're better—"

"Nonsense," her grandmother said, smiling at her from the hospital bed. "There's no point in wasting any time. Every day may count for you, Sarah darling. Life is too precious, believe me, I know. There's no need for you to stay here and hold my hand; you go out and fight for your own life. Follow this up, right away!"

When visiting time was up, Sarah went back outside, ready to share the news about the letter with her mom. But finding her mother virtually asleep in the uncomfortable plastic chair changed her mind.

"You've got to get some rest," Sarah insisted. "Why don't you come home with us? You're too sleepy to drive that far by yourself."

"I can't leave yet; anyhow, my car is here," her mother said, straightening with an obvious effort.

"I'll stay tonight if you go get some sleep," Sarah offered.

"No, I want you to get plenty of rest, and believe me, this waiting room is not built for comfort."

They argued for a few minutes, then Margaret Davenport agreed to go to a nearby motel for the night so that she could get some sleep, but only if Sarah let Mark drive her back home as planned.

This was not the time to tell her about the letter,

Sarah decided. Her mother was too tired to think and had too much anxiety to make well-balanced decisions.

They walked out to the parking garage together, after Margaret left a message with the nurses' desk about where she could be contacted. Mark transferred the bag with her mother's clothes to her mom's car, and they followed her to the motel parking lot, on Sarah's insistence.

Not until her mom was safely inside the motel room did Mark pull back into the street and head for the freeway.

"We'll have you home in a couple of hours," he told her. "You'll be in bed by ten. What are you going to do about the letter? I gather you decided not to tell your mom."

"Not now." She told him what her grandmother had said. "And she's right; I don't want to waste time."

"Are you going to call on your own?"

Sarah thought of the plane, winging its way through the blue sky. "I have her address, not her phone number."

"You can try information," Mark pointed out.

"I'm doing more than that." She sat up straighter against the car seat, excited at the thought of once more taking an active part in her own fight. "I'm going to find my birth mother. I'm going to Tennessee!"

Chapter
Six

Dear Diary,

Mark thinks I've gone loco. We argued all the way to Los Angeles, but I wouldn't change my mind, and he finally agreed to help. As soon as we got home, I went to my room and pored over my atlas. I studied the Tennessee map, then called the airport to check on the next flight to Tennessee, and threw some clothes into a duffel bag. I've left a note for Mrs. Wong, and also for my mother, and I'll call Mom once I get to Tennessee. But nothing is going to change my mind, not now. I might actually find my birth mother, someone who would be compatible as a bone marrow donor. This could be the difference between life and death. I can't sit here and wait, I just can't!

Sarah shut her diary and added it to the clothes and cosmetics in her bag. She picked up her stuffed lion, and glanced at last year's school yearbook. If she found her birth mother, maybe she'd want to see some of Sarah's activities in school, get some idea of her life. Then she zipped the canvas bag shut. She checked her watch for the tenth time in fifteen minutes, then turned off her bedside lamp. Lying back against the pillows, she took a deep breath and tried to relax. Sleep was impossible, she was too excited, too tense. The answer to all her questions, the gift of life itself, might lie at the end of her journey—how could anyone expect her not to go and find out for herself?

The apartment was very quiet; Mrs. Wong had retired to the master bedroom even before Sarah. Sarah could hear the hum of the refrigerator from the kitchen, and occasional sounds of traffic on the avenue outside their apartment building—all the usual sounds that she usually didn't even notice. But tonight she was conscious of everything. Finally she heard what she had been listening for—quiet, even breathing from the next bedroom, and in a few minutes even a soft, ladylike snore that made Sarah grin.

Good. If Mrs. Wong hadn't gone to sleep early, she had no idea how she would have gotten out of the apartment without any argument. But she would have gone, she had no doubt.

At eleven o'clock, Sarah got out of bed—she had never undressed—picked up her bag and her purse, and tiptoed to the apartment door. Opening it quietly, she stepped outside, then eased it shut and locked it again behind her.

Then she ran lightly down to the parking lot. Mark was waiting, frowning a little as he opened the door for her.

"Are you sure you won't change your mind?" His tone was worried.

She shook her head. "Why should I? My grandmother told me not to waste any time. I have to see what I can find out, and I can do much more if I'm there in person."

"But what if you get too tired, if you get sick—"

"If I get sick, I'll go to a doctor or even a hospital—I assume they do have them in Tennessee." Sarah knew that sounded too sarcastic; she took a deep breath. "Mark, I feel better right now than I have in a month; that's the truth. Just knowing there's hope—that I may find what I need—has given me more energy than I've had in ages. Trust me; this is the right thing for me to do."

"I hope so," Mark murmured, but his frown had lifted. He turned into the freeway and drove them through the lighter late-night traffic toward the airport. In less than half an hour, he pulled the car into the Los Angeles airport.

"You don't have to wait," she told him.

"Oh, yes, I do," he said firmly. "If I have to face your mom later, the very least I can tell her is that I saw you safely onto the plane and didn't leave you all alone in LAX in the middle of the night."

"I'm not a kid," she protested. But though she wouldn't admit it to him, she felt a reassuring warmth that Mark was determined to look out for her.

"Right, and how many plane trips have you taken lately?"

She grinned reluctantly. None, not since that first trip she had taken across country as an infant, with her new parents, to her new home.

Would this second flight of her life bring her back to her first home, her birth parents, the donor that she needed; was it all going to work out, after all?

Please, God, she thought, let me find them, let me live.

They parked in the parking garage, then dodged taxicabs and shuttle buses as they crossed the traffic lanes to one of the big airport buildings. Together, they headed for the long airline counter and stood in line. Ahead of them a businessman with a briefcase and a hanging bag waited, his expression tired and bored. In front of him, a couple with a squirming toddler checked in a stroller and three bags.

In a few minutes Sarah stood at the front of the line, meeting the polite, incurious gaze of the lady in the white blouse and navy skirt.

"I need a ticket to Nashville, please," Sarah told her, trying to sound calm.

To her relief, the woman didn't ask her age, didn't ask if she had permission from her parents to be flying across the country. As if this happened all the time—maybe it did—the woman punched the keys of her computer terminal and pulled up the information.

"We have a flight leaving at twelve-thirty for Nashville, with one stop in Santa Fe," she said, and quoted the price.

Sarah swallowed hard at the amount and handed over the credit card—good thing her mom had a good credit rating—but how much was Sarah's life worth? If this worked, her mother wouldn't begrudge the money spent on the ticket, Sarah was certain. And if it didn't—no, she wouldn't think like that.

The credit card was accepted, the woman behind the counter printed out the ticket and told her the gate number. "Any bags to check?"

Sarah shook her head. She'd keep her duffel bag with her—it would fit in the baggage compartment overhead, according to the size chart at the end of the counter.

She accepted the ticket with a sense of unreality; despite her excited planning, this still seemed a little like a dream. Without trying to explain her feelings, she took Mark's hand—he felt solid and strong, and his grip reassured her—and they walked toward the gate.

After pausing to go through the metal detector, they stopped at the gift shop and Mark bought her a pack of gum. "Keeps your ears from popping as you go up and down," he explained, and also some cookies to tuck into her purse. "Don't let your blood sugar drop too much."

She smiled in appreciation of his concern. "You're very special, Mark Summers, anyone ever tell you that?"

"Only one person who matters," he murmured.

They stopped at an ATM, and Sarah used the credit card again to draw out $200 in cash; she hoped it would be enough, added to the hundred her mom had left when she went to Santa Barbara.

Sarah clutched his arm as they approached the gate. The plane was already boarding; she felt suddenly very frightened. She was jumping off the world she knew into a totally strange place, and what if she didn't find anyone, what if she got stuck, stranded in a far-off state?

She took a deep breath. There were always phones. Whatever happened, her mom would only be a phone call away, ready to offer help, and at the worst, to guide her back home. The thought gave her strength.

"You can still change your mind, you know," Mark seemed to guess her thoughts. "Cash in the ticket and get your money back. You don't have to go."

"Yes, I do; I'd hate myself if I gave it up now, just because I'm nervous," Sarah told him. "I'll be okay."

He put his arms around her, and Sarah clung to him, leaning into his healthy body, his strong arms. She wanted her own health back, her life opening up before her again, not closing down in a losing battle with this cursed disease.

She wouldn't give up without trying. Taking a deep breath, Sarah lifted her chin and stepped out of his arms. She smiled at Mark, then turned and walked toward the flight attendant who was collecting tickets.

The young woman took her ticket, tore the boarding pass in two, and gave her back the stub. Sarah clutched her duffel bag tightly, pushed her purse over her shoulder, and walked down the rounded tunnel to the plane.

Another flight attendant waited at the plane's entrance. Sarah glanced at the thick door that sat open, then, biting her lip nervously, stepped into the plane. The attendant checked her boarding pass, then nodded toward the back. "Twenty-three C," she told her brightly.

Trying to look as if she did this every day, Sarah made her way through the narrow aisle to the seat marked on her ticket. She put her duffel bag into the overhead baggage compartment, and found a small pillow and blanket in the next overhead bin.

The plane seemed only half full; she had no one sitting in the two seats beside her. Just as well, Sarah had no desire for anyone to notice just how nervous she was.

She sat down in the window seat and fastened her seat belt, then peered out the thick pane of the rounded window. Mark was inside somewhere, watching until the plane took off. He seemed far away, and she felt very much alone.

Sarah found a safety card in the pocket of the

seat in front of her and studied it anxiously; where was the nearest exit? She glanced around covertly, then, sure she had memorized the entire card, sat back and waited for the remaining passengers to find their seats.

The flight attendant made announcements and explained the safety features. Sarah watched closely, trying to pretend she was as blasé as most of the other passengers. The man across the aisle from her had already loosened his tie and stowed his briefcase and was dozing, his head against the wall of the plane.

Sarah envied his nonchalance. When the announcement came over the loudspeaker, "Flight attendants, prepare for takeoff," she tensed and gripped her armrests tightly as the plane taxied forward.

But the plane paused as they waited their turn to take off, and Sarah tried to breathe normally. She suddenly remembered the gum Mark had bought her, and reached into her purse to pull out a stick. The plane moved again as she thrust it into her mouth, and Sarah tensed once more.

They were moving, faster, faster, the plane was lifting—she felt her stomach lurch and she shut her eyes. When she opened them again, they were turning. Sarah stared out the window into blackness; the sea was dark and cold beneath them; the thought made her shudder. Then the plane turned again, and she could see the myriad lights of Los Angeles and all the other surrounding cities that merged into the great metropolis. The lights were white and yellow and sometimes red and green; streetlights defined the avenues, and store signs twinkled, cars moved on the streets and freeways. The city was beautiful, seen from high above, and it seemed to stretch on forever.

Sarah knew it well enough to know that the dark streets could be grimy, the alleys filled with menace. But from here, it sparkled like an immense jewel, and she felt a pang to be leaving it behind. This was the only home she had known—what would Tennessee be like?

And she wasn't even going to Nashville, which was a big enough city, she thought. She had to go another hundred miles to a small town that she could hardly find on her map.

"How are you going to get there," Mark had argued. "Rental cars are expensive, you know."

"There must be a bus," she'd countered. "Someone at the airport will know. There must be a way to travel."

"Sure, by horse and buggy, maybe," Mark had scoffed.

But he was just being contrary, Sarah told herself. Pleasant Hills might be small, but it was a modern town. How different could it be?

And to find her birth mother—maybe her father, maybe even, Sarah thought suddenly, half brothers and sisters? She'd never had a brother or a sister; she'd grown up as an only child. What would it be like to find another girl who looked like her, maybe shared her passion for chocolate chip cookies or her dislike of mushrooms?

The thought offered so many unconsidered possibilities that Sarah felt her head spin. She'd face it when it happened, she told herself. She hadn't even found the town yet, nor the woman who wrote the letter, much less her birth mother. That was where it all began—the woman who'd given birth to Sarah—she was the key, the most essential element. First Sarah had to find the woman who'd given her away seventeen years ago, and hopefully the rest would follow.

Sarah found that her body was still rigid with tension, as if she were trying to hold the plane in the air by sheer willpower. In fact, the pilot and crew seemed to be doing just fine without her help.

She relaxed her grip on the armrests and leaned back. The man across the aisle had lifted the armrests, giving him the whole seat to lie across. Sarah found that her armrests could be lifted, too, and she made herself as comfortable with the pillow and blanket as she could. Wrapping the wad of gum into its foil paper, she shut her eyes.

Now that the first rush of excitement had passed, she felt very tired. Maybe a little sleep would be a good thing . . .

She slept and roused briefly when the plane landed and took off again in Santa Fe. She accepted a glass of orange juice from the attendant, then slept again, until a change in altitude made her ears ache. Sitting up, feeling lost and disoriented, she saw the attendants moving through the cabin. Where were they? Were they landing already?

She glanced at her watch; it was past four, and the darkness outside the plane window was lighter, gray merging into the pink softness of dawn. Confused, she looked at her watch again, then remembered the time change.

The FASTEN SEAT BELT light flashed on above her head, and Sarah hurried to adjust her seat belt. She stared out the window as the plane dropped lower. A whine outside the plane made her start, but when she glanced around, the other passengers looked stolid and unalarmed, so she assumed this was a normal sound. Turning back to the window, she saw thick patches of trees and scattered buildings beneath them. After the sweeping city they had left, she felt surprised at the empty countryside. Was it as primitive here as Mark had hinted?

No, now she saw streets and houses, and a glimpse of taller buildings. They were coming down rapidly, and Sarah braced herself without thinking. But the plane touched the runway with only a slight bump. She heard the noise of the plane braking, then its rapid speed slowed until they rolled closer to the airport building.

"Welcome to Nashville," the pilot said, his voice slightly muffled by the intercom. "Local time is six twenty-seven, temperature is seventy-four degrees. For passengers continuing on to Miami, we will be on the ground about thirty minutes . . ."

Sarah stopped listening. She was tense again, rigid with excitement and a trace of fear. This was it; she was in Tennessee. She wished fervently that her mother was with her, could take charge and find out how to get to this small town that she'd never before heard of. Why hadn't she waited for her mom to come with her?

Because every day mattered, every hour. She didn't have the time to spare. Sarah took a deep breath. The seat belt sign faded, and people were rising. She unfastened her seat belt and stood up, feeling stiff from the confined space and still tired despite her nap. Opening the overhead bin, she pulled out her duffel bag, made sure her purse was over her arm, and joined the line of passengers shuffling toward the exit.

This was it.

Chapter
Seven

Dear Diary,

I thought it would be so simple. I had a plan—why don't plans ever work the way you think they will? The Information Desk had no one there; a sign said someone would return in half an hour; I've waited 40 minutes already. I'm sitting in a plastic seat against the wall, feeling tired and hungry and very scared. What's my mom thinking now? I remember how much I used to dream about traveling. Now I just wish I were home in my own bedroom.

All she had seen of Tennessee so far was the Nashville airport, which was modern and clean and had posters of antebellum homes and thorough-bred horses and country singers. It also had hard plastic seats. Sarah sighed. She closed her diary, slipping it back into the duffel bag. Why didn't someone come?

She had stopped in the gift shop to buy a map of

Tennessee; she stared at the tiny dot that was Pleasant Hills one more time. What did it hold for her—answers to all her questions, or a dead end, in more ways than one?

A woman sat down next to her with a little baby in her arms; the infant was crying. The woman fussed over the baby, holding it to her shoulder and patting its back, finding a bottle of juice in the diaper bag and offering it to the baby. Finally, the wails ceased, and the infant sucked contently on the bottle.

Sarah wanted to yell, too. She thought again about calling her mom, but she kept putting it off. She was afraid that if she heard her mother's voice right now, she'd burst into tears, just like the baby next to her. That would really reassure her mother. Maybe she'd phone in a while, when she knew what she was going to do.

At last, a woman in a neat suit walked up to the small information kiosk and went inside. Sarah stood up quickly, grabbed her bag, and hurried up to the counter.

"I need to get to Pleasant Hills," she said, the words tumbling out quickly. "Can you tell me how to get a bus—can I get a bus?"

The woman pulled out bus schedules and flipped through them. She told Sarah where to find a bus to the main bus station; there she could buy a ticket to Pleasant Hills. Then, at Sarah's request, she repeated the directions again, and Sarah felt some of her panic subside.

"Thanks," she murmured, and slung her duffel over her shoulder. Maybe she'd make it after all.

She had to hurry to make the next bus to the depot; she caught it at the curb just as it was pulling out, climbed on, and paid the fare. The air outside the airport terminal felt thick with moisture, and warm. She felt perspiration drops on her forehead; she rubbed her face when she sat down.

Sarah had ridden the city buses in Los Angeles since she was twelve; she felt more at home on the bus than she had on the plane. Leaning back, she took a deep breath and stared out the window.

There seemed to be a lot of trees, even scattered around the city itself. And no palm trees, of course, these trees were lush and green and heavily leaved. The cars and trucks looked much the same, although the streets were not as broad or as multi-laned as in Los Angeles.

When they reached the main bus station, Sarah hurried to get off the bus and to stand in line at the ticket counter. When she bought her ticket, she found that she had almost an hour to wait. She picked up a bus schedule, then headed for the rest room. When she came out, she found a row of public phones. Using her mom's extra phone card, Sarah started to dial her home number, then hesitated. If Mrs. Wong was still there, she didn't want to hear any reproaches. She had the Santa Barbara hospital number in her purse; she called it instead, and when she reached the hospital information, she asked to leave a message for her mom. "Just tell her I arrived safely and will call later," she told the woman at the switchboard. "She'll know what I mean."

Then she hung up quickly, feeling both guilt at not speaking directly to her mom, and relief that there would be no confrontation, not yet. She was sure her mother would understand, but still—if Sarah learned something that would help her before she called again, her mom couldn't be angry or, worse, hurt that Sarah had worried her unnecessarily.

What about Mark? He'd be wondering about her, too. But she couldn't put too many long-distance calls on her mom's bill; Sarah was spending enough already. When she found out where she was staying—good question—Sarah would call him.

She went back to one of the benches and sat down, avoiding the ones with adjacent ashtrays. A thin man with dark, greasy hair eyed her; she felt her stomach knot with nervousness. But Sarah had grown up in a big city; she lifted her chin and frowned directly at him, her glance hostile.

He blinked and looked away first, and Sarah relaxed. She felt hungry; if there'd been a snack on the plane, she must have slept through it. She remembered the cookies Mark had bought for her. Warmed by his solicitude, she pulled them out of her purse and ate them quickly, washed down by a can of soda from a soft drink machine against the wall.

When she finished, she studied the map of Tennessee she had bought in the airport. The minutes dragged by; finally, they called her bus. The names blurred over the loudspeaker; Sarah listened anxiously to be sure. Yes, that was the one. She picked up her bag and walked quickly to board the big bus. It smelt a little stale inside, though she was relieved to see the NO SMOKING sign.

She showed the driver her ticket, then climbed up the steps and slid into a worn plush seat. This was it, the final stage of her journey.

By the time they pulled out into the street, the early morning traffic seemed to have abated. The big bus lumbered along in a stream of vehicles. It soon turned into an interstate, and Sarah craned her head to see the tall buildings at the city's center. Within a half hour, Nashville was behind them, and they rolled along past farm pastures and cornfields, where the cornstalks were taller than Sarah, topped with plump tasseled ears of corn, then more groves of thick trees. The interstate ran through rounded hills, with occasional layered walls of rock marking where the road had been cut through the hillside. Sarah stared at everything. This was the state in which she had been born; some part of her was here, had begun here. She wanted to see it all.

The driver turned on the radio, and a country song flowed past her. It was slow and sad, and it made her uncomfortable—she didn't need anyone's else sorrow right now; she had enough of her own. Sarah was relieved when the song ended and another tune came on; this one was more lively, faster paced. The lyrics said something about a cheating husband, but the woman's voice was confident and sassy, not at all gloomy.

So Sarah watched the hills slide by, heavily forested or dotted with meadows and grazing cows, while she hummed the tune of a country song.

Eventually, the drone of the bus's tires on the highway and the gentle swaying motion lulled her into a light doze. But she was too anxious to sleep soundly, and when the bus pulled off the highway for its first stop, she woke at once.

But this was not her stop. She watched a couple of passengers climb off—an elderly black woman wearing a prim straw hat, a man in blue jeans— then the bus slid away from the storefront and headed back for the highway.

There were three more stops before Pleasant Hills, and Sarah found that she was chewing on her fingernails—a bad habit she'd finally given up when she was fourteen. She pulled her hand away and looked at her ragged nail with disgust. But the nervous tremors inside her stomach were hard to quell.

Then the bus pulled off the road again, and the driver called, "Pleasant Hills."

Staring out the bus window, Sarah saw only a service station and a small store; was this all there was to the town? Feeling a moment of panic— what if she were stuck here and couldn't find anyone she was searching for—Sarah had to take a deep breath. It took all her courage to pick up her bag and walk off the bus. No one else followed.

When the bus pulled away with a muffled roar, leaving a strong smell of diesel fumes in the air, Sarah felt almost light-headed. Fields stretched around the small service station, and a narrower road ran off into the distance. She pushed her bag over her shoulder and walked into the store.

"Can I help you?" the lady at the cash register said. Her voice had an unfamiliar twang, a bit like the singer on the radio.

"Is this Pleasant Hills? I mean, is this all of it?" Sarah blurted, then felt foolish when the woman chuckled.

"Lord, no, honey. The town's down the road a piece. You looking for someplace special?"

"I, yes, I guess," Sarah muttered. "Is it far; can I walk, I mean?"

The woman's wide mouth turned down at the question, and Sarah's chest tightened again.

"Three, four miles, a good enough stroll. Where you going, hon?"

"I—is there anyplace to stay? A motel, maybe, not too expensive?"

The cashier looked Sarah up and down; her faded blue eyes narrowed a bit; they were unexpectedly shrewd.

"There's a run-down motel between Pleasant Hills and Four Points, but I wouldn't recommend it. Lady I know runs a bed and breakfast, nice old house right in town, and not real expensive. Maybe you'd like that?"

"That sounds very nice," Sarah agreed, feeling some of the tension inside her ease. "Do you have her number?"

The woman nodded. She checked a small book —it took Sarah a moment to realize it was a phone book; compared to the Los Angeles directory, it was amazingly small and thin—then dialed.

"Janet? Got a young lady here who's interested in a room. You open?" She nodded at the voice in the receiver, then handed it across the counter to Sarah.

Sarah clutched the beige receiver tightly. "Hello?" she said uncertainly, feeling a little foolish. "You have a room available?"

"Sure thing," the cheerful voice on the other end responded. "How long'll you be staying, dearie?"

"I—I'm not sure, a few days," Sarah said.

"Forty-five dollars a night, with breakfast but no other meals," the woman said. "I'm on Main Street, just past the Methodist church, the big tan house with blue shutters. I got air-conditioning, too."

The air in the store was cool enough, but Sarah still grinned. "Good," she said. "I'll be there in a little while."

She hung up the phone feeling more cheerful. "Thank you for your help," she told the cashier.

"Can you tell me how to find the bed and break-fast?"

Now that she had a destination, she didn't feel as fearful of walking. But the woman shook her head.

"Just a minute."

The bell jingled as an elderly man opened the door and came inside. While Sarah talked on the phone, she had seen the pickup truck pull up outside, and the man get out and gas up, but she'd paid little attention. The man had graying hair and a neat blue shirt tucked into his jeans.

"Mac," the cashier said. "You heading back to town?"

He nodded, pulling out a twenty and handing it across.

She made change, then glanced back at Sarah. "This young lady's going to stay at Janet's bed and breakfast on Main Street. Think you could give her a lift?"

The man looked at Sarah for a moment, then answered slowly, "I reckon so. Let me check the oil, young lady, then I'll be heading out." Taking her acquiescence for granted, he walked back outside.

Surprised, Sarah opened her mouth to protest, then hesitated. Accepting rides from strangers was high on her childhood list of forbidden behaviors.

But the cashier seemed to read her thoughts. "You look a mite peaked, and it's a good four miles. I've known Mac all my life; don't you fret about him."

She smiled, and Sarah grinned weakly. Her mother wouldn't approve, but Sarah trusted the woman's friendliness. "Thanks a lot."

She walked outside and approached the truck cautiously. Mac had already wiped oil off the dipstick and checked the measurement, then he slammed the hood down. "Climb in," he told her.

Sarah opened the far door and took a seat in the truck, sitting very close to the door. When Mac got behind the wheel and pulled out, he turned away from the highway.

As he drove past more green fields, some yellowed and short as if already harvested, he glanced at her curiously. "Staying long?"

"I'm not sure," Sarah murmured, not meeting his eyes. To her relief, buildings soon appeared, a Dairy Dip and a small hardware store, a grocery, then a row of old Victorian frame homes with elaborate wood trim, some in good shape, some with paint peeling and shutters sagging. Brick buildings held a small bank and more shops. They were already on Main Street, Sarah saw, maybe it was the town's only main avenue.

Mac turned into a driveway, and she saw the small sign on the lawn: PLEASANT HILLS BED AND BREAKFAST. It was another of the big old homes, but happily, it looked well maintained. The exterior was painted a light tan, and the doors and shutters were dark blue. Flowers bloomed in window boxes, and lace curtains hung at the window.

Sarah climbed quickly out of the truck, charmed by the picture. "Thank you for the ride," she told the old man, and he nodded.

"Anytime."

He pulled away, and Sarah walked slowly to the front door and pushed the button.

She heard the doorbell peal, and in a moment footsteps inside, then the door opened. Sarah stood face-to-face with a plump woman with up-swept hair. Her brown eyes had laugh lines at the corners, and she had a round, cheerful face.

"Welcome," she said. "Come on in; my name's Janet Williams. I got a nice room all ready."

She showed Sarah through the front hall and into a big room with an old-fashioned white iron bed and a heavy dark-colored bureau. A small television sat on a table across the room, and the windows looked out toward the street; Sarah could see a car drive past, and a sidewalk that led far-ther into town. The thick quilt on the bed was a patchwork of cheerful prints, and pink roses were scattered across the wallpaper. It would be like sleeping in a summer garden, Sarah thought.

Her landlady was waiting, her expression expec-tant.

"It's very pretty," Sarah told her.

"I'm glad you like it. It's forty-five dollars a night, as I said, the first night in advance, please."

Sarah fumbled with her purse, a little awkward

with the business end of things. She counted out the money carefully, and Mrs. Williams seemed to relax.

"Is there a phone?" Sarah asked, glancing around.

"There's a pay phone in the sitting room; I had a little trouble with people making long-distance calls," the landlady explained. "Breakfast is from eight to ten; you just let me know when you want it, dear."

She went out of the room and closed the door behind her. Sarah glanced into the adjoining bathroom, with its clean pink towels and old-fashioned tub. She washed her face and hands, feeling both relieved and nervous all over again.

Now to find the woman who had written her the letter, and convince her to tell Sarah just who her birth mother might be.

And if Mary Anne wouldn't tell?

Sarah took a deep breath. She had to, that's all. Sarah wouldn't leave here without knowing, not when she'd come so far, not when the answer was so close. If there was any chance of stopping her cancer, she had to find it.

Chapter

Eight

Dear Diary,

I rested awhile; now I'm sitting on the bed trying to get up enough nerve to call Mary Anne
Barnes, the woman who wrote me the letter. I'm
trying to think of the right words to say to her.
I'm afraid I'll be so scared I'll forget everything I
want to ask. And what will I do if she won't tell
me who she thinks my birth mother might be?
I'm so nervous . . .

Sarah put down her diary; she was stalling, and
it wasn't going to get any easier. Taking the letter
out of her purse, she stood up and headed for the
sitting room of the bed and breakfast. The sitting
room was easy to find; it was on the front side of
the house, and they had passed it going to her bedroom. Plump chairs and a skirted sofa filled the
sunny room, and an ancient piano sat at one end.
Sarah walked in; no one else was in the room,
and that was just as well. She looked around and

spotted the telephone on the side, with a big wicker chair sitting beside it. She hurried over to the phone, perched on the edge of the chair, and picked up the directory from the table beside the chair.

She flipped through the pages quickly; there were two Barnes listed in the phone book, but neither was Mary Anne. Now what? Okay, stay calm, Sarah told herself. The listing was probably under her husband's number. She'd just have to call each number; at least, there weren't a hundred people with this last name as there would have been in Los Angeles.

She found a coin in her purse and dialed the first number listed, Robert Barnes. The phone rang, while Sarah clutched the receiver very tightly, and rang again. She was so tense she almost couldn't breathe, but the ringing continued with no answer. No one home.

Disappointed, she pushed the lever down, and her quarter slipped back out into the change slot. Sarah tried the next number, George Barnes, and this time a voice answered on the third ring.

"Hello?"

"Hello," Sarah said, almost whispering. "Is—is Mary Anne there?"

"Speak up, I can't hear you."

"Is Mary Anne there, please?"

"You got the wrong number," the querulous voice said; it sounded like a very old woman.

Sarah swallowed hard; her hopes, which had

been rising rapidly, sank just as fast. She wanted to cry and had to fight to hold back a sob.

But like an answer to an unspoken prayer, the old lady went on, "Mary Anne's at the tearoom this time of day, anyhow."

"Thank you," Sarah said quickly before the connection was broken.

Tearoom? There was nothing listed under Barnes that mentioned a tearoom. She flipped the pages back to the M's, and found Mary Anne's Tearoom listed in bold print.

And it was on Main Street. Well, most of the town was, as far as Sarah had seen. She looked at the address again, and her heart beat faster. It couldn't be that far from here. If she went in person, maybe it would be harder for Mary Anne to say no to her, to refuse to talk or answer questions.

Making a quick decision, Sarah put the phone book back on the table and jumped up, her purse over her arm. She headed for the front door, out the short walk, then hesitated. She hadn't seen a tearoom on her drive in, so it must be farther toward the center of this tiny town.

She turned left and walked rapidly down the old sidewalk, its cracked cement buckling in places from the pressure of tree roots. Sarah looked around at the big houses that lined the street, their Victorian facades adorned with fanciful trim. The yards were large and green, the tall trees leafy, their shade pleasant on a warm day. Once a pickup truck drove past, but the street was quiet compared to the busy avenues she saw at home. And the gracious, if sometimes shabby, old houses looked little like the stucco apartment building where Sarah and her mom lived. Instead of orange bird-of-paradise flowers, pink roses grew up a trellis against the nearest house.

She saw small election signs in some of the yards; Wilson for mayor, Smith for sheriff, Wright for state representative. Even the sky was different, somehow a softer, more muted blue, and the clouds were big and fluffy, not like the wispy cirrus clouds she was accustomed to seeing over the southern California landscape.

It made Sarah feel very lonely. And yet some part of her should know this place—perhaps she had been born near here, had lived here a few days until the woman who bore her had sent her away. Probably for her own good, Sarah told herself. Probably for an excellent reason. Yet she couldn't feel any link with this small town or its quiet street. Her connection, like the umbilical cord, had been severed too long ago.

Two more blocks, then she saw more businesses, a small drugstore, a dress shop, an antique store, then a small city hall and sheriff's office, with a patrol car sitting in front. Many of the stores were old, and some were empty, with dusty windows and locks on the door.

Then she saw it, an old brick building with a bright-colored sign in the window, and red-checked café curtains covering the bottom part of the front window. MARY ANNE'S TEAROOM, the sign said, HOURS 10:00 TO 6:00.

Sarah took a deep breath, then pushed the heavy wooden door and walked in. The air was slightly cooler than outside, and carried the fragrant smell of pastries. Sarah felt her stomach rumble. There were small tables at each side of the room, and a glass case toward the back whose shelves held cakes and pies and plates of scones and cookies. Two women sat at one of the tables, talking and eating, and a potbellied man in a business suit read his newspaper at another, drinking a cup of coffee, his plate pushed back.

Sarah walked in slowly and on to the bakery case at the end of the room. For a moment, no one seemed to notice her, then a young woman came through with a pot of coffee. She smiled briefly at Sarah, then refilled the businessman's cup.

Returning to the case, she said, "May I help you? Would you like a table?"

Sarah shook her head. "Not yet," she said. "I'd like to speak to Mary Anne, please." This couldn't be Mary Anne; surely she was much too young to have any memories of a seventeen-year-old adoption?

"She's in the kitchen. If you'll hang on a sec, I'll tell her."

She disappeared through swinging doors, and Sarah waited, trying to be patient, though she wanted to shout, instead. To be this close, and not know the answer—it was all she could do to stand quietly and not bite her nails again.

The woman who came out next was middle-aged, stout, with a pretty pink apron covering her slacks and cotton top. She had a sensible, pleasant face, adorned with little makeup, and her eyes were intelligent.

Sarah had a fleeting thought that if this had been her birth mother, she would not have been disappointed. "Hello," she said. "I'm Sarah Davenport. You wrote in answer to my letter in the paper, about the adopted baby."

Mary Anne's eyes widened in surprise. She looked around at the half-empty tearoom, then nodded briskly toward the back. "Why don't you come into the kitchen," she said, a little loudly. "I have a new batch just about to come out of the oven."

Sarah blinked, but she followed her through into the inner room. The air was warmer, here. The kitchen looked clean, if a trifle cluttered; it was a small narrow room, the big table filled with trays of cooling scones. Boxes of different teas lined the back counter, and there were pans in the sink waiting to be washed.

"You're the girl with cancer?" Mary Anne looked her up and down. "Well, you do look a mite pale. I never thought you'd come here." She sounded somewhat alarmed at the unexpected result her letter had produced. "I just thought you'd write back, you know."

Sarah shrugged. "I don't have any time to waste," she tried to explain. "It's so important. I can't wait too long, and I have to find a donor. Please, can you tell me who the mother was of the baby who was adopted, so I can try to find out if that baby was me?"

Mary Anne hesitated, wiping her hands on her apron. She looked away from Sarah's pleading face. "I hate to be a gossip," she murmured, her tone uncertain. "And what if it's not the right baby, after all?"

A timer beeped, and she turned away to pull open the oven door and remove another tray of cookies. Sarah watched her move briskly from the big stove to the table with its racks, and her heart sank. If Mary Anne wouldn't tell her what she knew, the trail could die here.

"Please," she said quietly. "You were willing to help me when you wrote the letter. Nothing has changed. I don't want to die, and I need your help."

Mary Anne paused, bending over the table, then straightened slowly. "I just hate to cause any trouble," she said, the indecision on her face lingering.

"I'll be as discreet as I can; I don't want to be a problem for anyone, honest," Sarah told her. "But I need a name, the mother of that baby. Please?"

Sarah knew her expression was strained; Mary Anne glanced at her once, then away. If she said no, Sarah was afraid the tears just behind her eyelids would overflow. If she had come all this way for nothing . . .

"All right, but don't you tell who told you," Mary Anne suddenly gave in. She tore a sheet of paper from the notepad on the counter and wrote, handing it to Sarah.

Sarah glanced at it, saw a name, "Ellen Mac-Pherson," but no address or phone number. She looked back up at Mary Anne.

"I went to high school with her," she explained. "That's how I knew about the baby. But I haven't spoken to her in years, and that's the truth." Yet she didn't meet Sarah's desperate gaze; was she lying, after all?

How would Sarah ever find Ellen if she had moved away from this small town, maybe even out of the state? Disappointment lay heavy inside her, a weight that robbed her of all the energy that hope and excitement had given her. She suddenly felt very tired; it was an effort just to stand.

"Thank you for this," she murmured. She tucked the scrap of paper into her jeans pocket, as if Mary Anne might change her mind and take this back, too. "If I can find her, you may have saved my life."

Mary Anne frowned. "Good luck," she said, but she had already turned back to her baking.

Sarah walked slowly out of the kitchen. She still felt leaden with the weight of her disappointment; she had headed for the door when a sudden cramping in her stomach reminded her of how hungry she was. But she couldn't bear to sit here; she was too close to tears. Still, she needed to eat.

She wheeled and went back to the glass case; the young woman was taking money from the man who had finally finished his coffee and his newspaper. When she pushed the cash drawer on the cash register shut, she turned to Sarah.

"Could I have two scones to go, please?" She pointed toward the case. "Yes, the cinnamon."

She paid for the pastries, accepted the paper bag, then hurried outside and headed for the bed and breakfast. Walking quickly, she took out one of the scones and bit into it. It tasted sweet and good; she soon had crumbs on her chin and T-shirt.

Sarah had gulped it down before she reached the bed and breakfast, and paused to brush the crumbs off before she went inside. The hollowness inside her stomach had eased a little, but the bigger emptiness inside was unabated. She went to her room, dropped her purse, and fell across her bed. At last the tears came, dripped unheeded down her cheeks. She sobbed aloud, then put one hand over her mouth in case someone should hear her.

Why had she thought it would be so easy? Just fly in, pick up the name and number, introduce yourself to the woman who had given birth to you but then walked out of your life, a woman who didn't seem in any hurry to be found. But Sarah had so little time. She put her head down and cried until the pillow was damp beneath her cheek.

Then, exhausted, she slept. When she woke, the afternoon sunshine slanted across the brightly colored quilt, and her head ached dully. She pushed herself up and glanced into the mirror; her eyes were swollen and her cheek had a red mark on it where she had lain on a wrinkle in the cotton pillowcase. She felt dull and discouraged. Now what? Give up and fly back to California, wait for someone else to find an answer, if there was one?

No, she refused to do that. She wouldn't give up; it was Sarah's life on the line, and she wasn't going to sit by, no matter how tired and wretched she felt, how hopeless the situation seemed.

She took the precious scrap of paper out of her jeans pocket and examined it more closely. Was this her birth mother? If she could locate this woman, would she finally find out all the answers to the questions she had pushed to the back of her mind? Would she find a key to a new life?

Sarah wouldn't give up, not yet.

Chapter
Nine

Dear Diary,

I'm back to the needle in the haystack, except maybe this time it's a bigger needle. I have her name, that's something, this mysterious woman who gave up a baby to be adopted. Ellen MacPherson: is she the right woman, am I her baby? I have to find her, and quickly; the sands are still drifting through the hourglass—I can see it in my mind. If I don't find a donor, I'm going to die. And I don't know where to start.

Sarah put her diary away; she felt calmer now that she had written down her fears. And without the fear, her mind worked more smoothly; finally, a thought came.

She ran out of the bedroom and back to the front room with its phone book. She flipped through the pages—MacPherson. But there was no listing.

Disappointed, Sarah replaced the directory and

went back to her rented bedroom. She wasn't all
that hungry, but she knew she needed to eat; the
nurses had talked to her about proper nutrition.
She needed to find some food. Not back to the
tearoom, she didn't want to see Mary Anne again,
at least not right now. But there had to be somewhere else to eat in this town.

Sarah grabbed her purse and headed out the
door again. She'd seen a small fast-food restaurant
a few blocks up; she walked slowly until she saw
the Dairy Dip, a tiny white block building with several cars and a rusty pickup truck in the parking
lot.

She bought a hamburger and some fries, and a
thick chocolate milk shake. She'd meant to sit
down on one of the picnic tables at the side, but a
teenaged boy in the pickup truck winked and
grinned at her as she walked past.

Sarah wasn't in the mood for silly come-ons. But
a thought made her pause, and she walked closer
to the truck.

"Hi, Gorgeous. You're new around here, aren't
you?" He wore a T-shirt with a rock band's logo
on the front and faded jeans. Except for the accent
and the Vol ball cap pulled low on his forehead, he
could have been any California teen.

Not exactly a brilliant opening line, Sarah
thought. But she smiled at him anyhow. "Yes, I
am. I'm looking for a woman named Ellen Mac-
Pherson, who used to live in Pleasant Hills. Have
you heard of her?"

He shook his head. "Nope, sorry. But I know lots of other people. Why don't you sit in the truck with me and talk awhile?"

Sarah wasn't that dedicated to her detecting; besides, she doubted that he would know anything helpful.

"Sorry," she said, shook her head. "Got to go."

But that meant she couldn't sit down in front of the Dairy Dip. Sarah carried her bag of food and walked past the parking lot.

Set back from the street was a large two-story brick building. The paint on the trim was faded, and strands of ivy clung to the walls, which were spotted with age. PLEASANT HILLS SCHOOL, the sign said. GRADES K–8.

Sarah felt a prickling of excitement; Mary Anne had said that she went to high school with Ellen MacPherson. Where was the high school, and would anyone there still remember who Ellen was, and where she might be today? At least it was a place to start.

First, she had to eat. Sarah sat down on the brick wall surrounding the school and slowly chewed on the burger and fries, managing to eat most of the food, then finished her milk shake.

She put her trash into the bag and carried it up the walk toward the school until she found a trash can. Then she walked to the main entrance and went through the double doors.

The school had the familiar smell of books and chalk dust and cleaning fluid. The clock on the wall read three-thirty, and Sarah heard someone talking inside a classroom, but the hallway was empty; littered with a couple of dropped papers. Classes had let out for the day, and soon the teachers would be leaving, too. Sarah hurried down the hallway.

A sign pointed to the main office, and Sarah walked inside. A young woman in a white blouse and gray skirt, her blond hair neatly pulled back and held by a small bow, sat behind the counter. She looked up. "Can I help you?"

"I'm actually looking for the local high school," Sarah told her.

"Oh, that's the county high school, about ten miles outside of town."

Sarah's hopes dropped. Ten miles was a long way when you didn't have any transportation. Was there a local bus? She'd have to find out.

"I'm looking for old high school annuals and any records that might remain from the early seventies," she told her.

The young secretary raised her brows.

"I'm doing some genealogy research," Sarah explained quickly. "Looking for information about family, you know." That part was true enough, Sarah thought.

The young woman nodded. "Oh, sure. As a matter of fact, we might have some old annuals in our library. I think Mrs. Elliot is still here, you can walk down and ask her, if you like; it's at the end of the hall. As for any records, they'd be at the county superintendent's office."

Sarah thanked her and hurried down the hall to find the library, hoping the librarian hadn't gone home. When she saw the big room with book-shelves lining the wall, she pulled open the glass-paned door and walked inside.

At first she thought that the library was empty, then she heard sounds from a small room at the back. Sarah walked closer; it was an office, and a woman in her midtwenties was checking files.

Sarah had hoped for an older woman who might remember a student from two decades ago; this woman obviously wasn't old enough.

Mrs. Elliot looked at her in surprise. "Can I help you?"

"I spoke to the lady in the front office," Sarah said. "She thought you might have some old high school annuals from the seventies. I'm doing some family research, and I wanted to look through the pictures."

The librarian nodded slowly. "As a matter of fact, we do have some. This used to be the old high school, you know, and when they moved to the new building, they didn't move all the old books. They're on the bottom shelf in the corner."

Sarah followed eagerly, then knelt down to look through the faded books.

"I'll be locking up at four o'clock," Mrs. Elliot said. "You can look at them until then; I'm afraid we don't check those out to anyone."

She had forestalled Sarah's question. Sarah nodded. "Thank you." She'd just have to make the most of the twenty minutes she had.

There was an index in the back of each volume, so it wasn't necessary to flip through the whole book. Starting in 1980, Sarah worked her way backward. In the '78 annual she found the name she was after, and her eyes widened.

Ellen MacPherson, page 44. Sarah flipped through the pages, then drew in her breath sharply. Ellen had long straight seventies' hair and a small smile; she looked young in the photo, and very vulnerable. And she looked a little like Sarah, the same curved brows, the full lower lip.

It made Sarah feel very strange, looking at this girl who might be her birth mother. But there was nothing in the high school annual to denote her address, still less where she might have gone after high school.

The librarian was putting on her suit jacket; Sarah stood up slowly. "Thank you for letting me look at the books," she said.

"I hope they were helpful," Mrs. Elliot said.

"Yes," Sarah said. But she still had a long way to go.

They walked out of the building side by side, and Sarah pulled herself together enough to ask, as she followed the librarian out the double doors, "Do you know of any MacPhersons still in this area?"

Mrs. Elliot pursed her lips. "Seems to me there's

an old lady with that name in the nursing home. My great-grandmother is there, so I visit when I can."

Sarah felt a surge of excitement. "Thanks," she said. "Where is this place, exactly?"

"Turn off Main Street onto Second Avenue, and go about three blocks."

Another lead—and Sarah would never forget the face she had seen in the yearbook. In that high school photo, Ellen was hardly older than Sarah was right now; could she already have had the baby that had been placed for adoption?

Sarah thought about having a baby at seventeen, about the responsibility that would go on and on forever, having a helpless infant dependent on you all the time. You'd have to know so much, and she knew nothing about babies. How could any teenager cope?

Had Ellen been afraid, much as Sarah was now, though for different reasons? Had she lain awake at night, too, wondering what was the best course to take? Thinking about her like that, confused and uncertain, it was easier for Sarah to understand why Ellen might have given up the baby.

Sarah walked back to the street; her shoulders sagged from fatigue, and her legs felt weak. But she refused to stop now. She had another clue, and if this old woman should know Ellen, know where she might be found today, Sarah could call her, check her identity, ask her the crucial questions.

She walked slowly down Main Street until a

small street sign alerted her to Second Avenue. It was an even smaller street, lined by comfortable frame or brick houses, older homes with rose-bushes in the yards, and flower beds filled with pansies. It all looked so settled, so quiet and peaceful. What would she have been like if she had been raised here? Sarah wondered. How different would she be?

It was a disturbing question. She wanted her own life, she wanted to be herself, no one else. And no way would she ever want to give up her mom, her grandmother, nor the memory of her dad. And what about Mark and Maria and her other friends? No, she'd remain Sarah Daven-port, thank you very much.

Her legs felt rubbery by the time she saw the long, low building that housed the nursing home. Would they ask her who she was and why she wanted to see the old lady?

Sarah walked up to the front door. It was locked, but a small sign told her to punch in a code, 1-2-3-4, on the keypad, and the door opened to her touch. Inside the lobby, the chairs were comfortable and the prints on the wall cheerful. But the elderly people who sat and stared at the door, waiting for visitors perhaps, or just breaking the monotony of the day, made Sarah hesitate. One little lady with blue-gray hair smiled up at Sarah, and Sarah smiled back. An old man in a wheelchair, his mouth sunken in around toothless gums, waved at her, as if unable to talk, and she smiled at him, too. But the sharp hospital smell of antiseptic made her wrinkle her nose, and Sarah headed for the nursing station past the front hall.

"I'm looking for Mrs. MacPherson," Sarah told the white-clad woman behind the counter.

"Room 112," the nurse told her, barely glancing up. "To your left."

Relieved, Sarah hurried down the hall, her weariness almost forgotten. She slowed her steps when she passed another elderly resident in a wheelchair, feeling somehow guilty for being able to walk without impediment.

But here it was, Room 112, and the name on the door said Mrs. Adelia MacPherson. Sarah looked cautiously inside.

A tiny woman, her back hunched, her face surrounded by wisps of white hair that escaped the bun on the back of her head, sat in a chair by the window, watching a bird feeder outside the windowpane.

Sarah didn't know whether to knock. "Excuse me," she said. "May I come in?"

But the little woman smiled and motioned her inside.

"My name is Sarah Davenport," she said. "Are you Mrs. MacPherson?"

The elderly lady nodded. "I have a robin today," she said happily. "And two redbirds, and a nuthatch. And lots of sparrows, of course, but I don't mind them."

Sarah looked outside the window at the bird

feeder, and the birds that fluttered around the tray of seeds. She could see the flash of red among the feathered diners. "It's very nice," she agreed.

She sat down gingerly on the side of the narrow bed. At least, Mrs. MacPherson didn't seem to mind having a stranger coming to visit.

"Mrs. MacPherson." Sarah took a deep breath and plunged in. "I'm looking for an Ellen Mac-Pherson who graduated from the local high school about 1978; do you know her? I—I think I might be related to her."

"Oh, Ellen, nice girl." The old lady nodded wisely, then looked back outside the window.

Sarah held her breath—was it going to work, after all? "Where is she now, do you know?" she asked quickly.

Mrs. MacPherson didn't seem to hear. "Had a bluejay earlier, but don't like him," she said, her voice sharper. "Drove the other birds away, greedy thing, he is!"

"Mrs. MacPherson, could you tell me where Ellen is living now?" Sarah repeated, raising her voice. Maybe the old woman was a little deaf.

"What?"

"Ellen MacPherson, can you tell me where she's living now?"

"She hasn't brought me any more bird seed," the old woman complained.

Sarah blinked in confusion. Did Ellen come to visit? But from how far away?

"Where does she live?"

"Who?"

"Ellen, Mrs. MacPherson. Where does Ellen live?" she was almost shouting now, trying to get through to the old lady.

"Need more sunflower seeds," Mrs. MacPherson muttered, pulling her sweater closer around her shoulders. "My robin likes sunflower seeds. She should bring me more."

Sarah felt her hopes plummeting all over again. "Mrs. MacPherson, do you know a girl named Mary?" she asked, deliberately testing.

"Nice girl, Mary," the old woman murmured, looking at the birds.

It was hopeless. If this frail little woman did know Ellen, the secret was well locked inside the fractured kaleidoscope of her memory.

Sarah thought she might cry. "Have a nice time with your birds," she murmured politely. "Thank you anyhow."

She walked to the door; the old woman paid no attention to her leaving. Sarah went slowly down the hall, feeling as if she'd walked a hundred miles today, and all for nothing.

At the nurse's desk, she paused again. "Can you tell me who Mrs. MacPherson's closest relatives are?" she asked the nurse behind the counter.

"We don't give out that kind of information," the nurse told her, her glance sharp and suspicious.

"I see." Sarah shrugged and headed for the outer door. Again, she had to punch a code to get out, and she was glad to feel the fresh air on her face, to leave the sour smells of the nursing home behind. She'd been so hopeful! Now, she still had to walk back to the bed and breakfast, and she'd never been so tired.

What had she accomplished with this wild trip across the country? Nothing, really. She had a name, a youthful image in her mind, but if she couldn't find the woman who belonged to the face in the old yearbook, what good would it do?

And the sand still flowed through the hourglass.

Chapter
Ten

Dear Diary,

I can't believe I've only been in Tennessee one day; it seems like a month. I still don't have any clues as to where I might find this woman who might be my birth mother. I'm tired, and I think my fever is back; I feel hot and sticky. Has this all been a wild goose chase? And I need to call Mom and Mark. I feel totally defeated.

Sarah closed her diary and lay back across the bed; she was exhausted, and she felt terrible. She reached for her shoulder bag, poked through the purse until she found her antibiotics—had she forgotten to take one this morning?—and some Tylenol. The leukemia reduced the strength of her immune system and left her vulnerable to any infection. The doctor had prescribed antibiotics for her to take, and the Tylenol would help control the fever; at least, she hoped it would.

There were some paper cups in the bathroom;

Sarah swallowed the pills and looked at the bath-
tub longingly. She felt hot and tired and grungy,
and a bath might make her feel better, and could
help lower the fever, too. But she was almost too
tired to even run the water.

Sighing, she turned on the water, adjusted it to
slightly warm, and let it run while she stripped off
her jeans and T-shirt and underwear. She stepped
into the tub and lay back, relaxing in the soothing
feel of the water.

For a few minutes she just lay there, her head
against the hard porcelain of the old tub, then, before the tub became too full, she stuck her head
under the tall spigot and washed her hair.

Were more strands falling out? Maybe not.
Sarah slicked her wet hair back out of her face and
turned off the water. She soaped and rinsed her
body, touching the small scar on her upper chest
where the peripheral intravenous central catheter
had been inserted four years ago, so that the IV
and chemo could be run into a tube inserted into
her chest, leading directly to a vein. It saved her
the endless pain and probing of needles, but it had
to be cleaned and flushed daily, and Sarah had
hated it, a constant reminder of her condition.
She'd had it removed during her last remission,
but she'd soon have to have it put back, either for
the bone marrow transplant, if that ever took
place, or for more chemo. Unless she just stayed
home and waited to die. Sometimes that seemed
like the easiest thing to do.

Then Sarah thought of her mother, and had to blink hard. She didn't want to leave her mom alone; how would her mother cope with losing first a husband, and then her only daughter? Because she was Margaret Davenport's daughter, not this unknown woman, wherever she was. Sarah blinked back a stray tear, and then sat up, feeling a flicker of determination return. She wasn't ready to give up, not yet.

She pushed herself up from the tub, pulled the plug to drain the water, and reached for a towel. She dried herself quickly, towel-drying her short hair and pushing it into place with her fingers. She pulled on clean underwear from her bag and a pair of shorts and a T-shirt. Then she picked up her purse and headed for the sitting room; she couldn't put it off any longer; she had to call home.

It was after eleven, but with the two-hour time difference, it would be only nine o'clock back in southern California. First she dialed Mark, hoping he was home. He answered quickly.

"Hello?"

"Mark, it's me."

"Geez, Sarah, I thought you'd never call. Are you okay?"

"I'm fine; I'm staying at a little bed and breakfast in Pleasant Hills, with a nice lady. I took a bus out here, no trouble at all."

"How do you feel? Have you found anything?"

"I have the name of my birth mother; I just don't know where to find her," Sarah explained.

"But I'm still looking. And I'm tired, but I'm always tired. I'd be tired if I were sitting at home," she added with a touch of bitterness.

She wouldn't say anything about her fever, which came and went most of the time, too. Anyhow, after the tepid bath and the tablets, she felt cooler.

"I wish I could be with you, Sarah," Mark told her; his tone was low and sincere. "I wish I could be more help; I hate to think of you out there all by yourself."

She felt comforted by his concern. "You have helped me," she told him. "And just knowing that you care—that makes me feel good. Have you talked to my mom?"

He groaned. "Of course, she called me when she read your note, and I felt like such a scumball."

"Is she really mad?" Sarah felt her pulse jump. "And how's my grandmother?"

"Your grandmother's okay, so far. And your mom was upset, but I think she's calmed down. You need to call her, Sarah. She's still at the hospital in Santa Barbara."

"I know." Sarah bit her lip, feeling tense with guilt. "I'd better go."

"Sarah? Take care of yourself, okay?"

"I will."

Before she could lose her nerve, Sarah punched in the numbers of the hospital, then her mom's phone card code.

This time, the hospital desk told her that her

grandmother had been moved to a private room. That was a good sign, surely? Did it mean her grandmother was recovering?

Sarah waited to be transferred to the hospital room, and after only one ring, she heard a familiar voice say anxiously, "Hello?"

"It's me, Mom," Sarah said, hating herself for the quiver she heard in her mother's voice.

"Oh, Sarah, thank God." There was a long sigh. "Are you all right?"

"I'm fine, honest." Sarah repeated the information she'd given to Mark. "The bed and breakfast is in this old Victorian house, really cute. You'd like it. And the lady who runs it is very nice and grandmotherly."

Her mother's tone sounded less tense, but she said wryly, with black humor, "If you weren't so sick, I'd strangle you myself, Sarah. I was so worried about you!"

"I know; I'm sorry. But I had to do something; I couldn't just sit there and wait," Sarah tried to explain. "I had to do something for myself."

"I understand, Sweetheart. I just wish you'd told me."

"If I'd told you what I wanted to do, you'd have said no," Sarah pointed out.

Her mother made a sound between a laugh and a groan. "I'm sure I would," she agreed. "Have you found out the name of your birth mother?"

"I know her name, Ellen MacPherson, if she's the right one, and I think she is," Sarah said. "I don't know where to find her yet, but I'm still look-ing."

"Sarah, I wish you'd come home. As soon as Nana is out of the hospital—she's getting stronger —we'll go out there together and look."

"I can't wait," Sarah said. "I don't know how much time I have; I just can't sit back and let it run out."

"Then I'll come out; I don't like you being there alone. I'll check on the plane schedules and—"

"No, Mom, Nana needs you there," Sarah ar-gued. "I'm okay, I really am." And maybe it would be easier to meet her birth mother alone, Sarah thought fleetingly. "I need to do this myself."

"But, Sarah—"

"If I start feeling sick, I'll call, and you could be here in a few hours." Her mother hesitated, and Sarah added, "I promise. Right now, I'm fine."

That wasn't true, and they both knew it. But Sarah could see the hourglass, with the sand run-ning. Just thinking about it made her stiff with fear.

"All right," her mom said. "But call me again tomorrow, please."

"Okay." Sarah gave her mother the name and number of the bed and breakfast, then sent love to her grandmother before she hung up the phone.

Feeling as if a weight had been removed from her shoulders, Sarah went slowly back to her room, pulled off her clothes, and crawled into bed.

Maybe tomorrow she'd think of something more to do, a way to find Ellen.

She slept restlessly, with dreams of babies and young girls, and everyone crying. Then it changed to an old nightmare, she was small, helpless, and someone was taking her away from her adopted parents, and she was screaming, "No, no," but no one listened.

She woke up sweating and almost sick with anxiety. A few years ago she had seen on television news reports a toddler being taken away from her adopted family by the courts and given back to her birth parents. The sight of the little girl screaming had haunted her for a long time. Sarah had had nightmares for weeks, thinking of being snatched up and taken away from the only home she knew, the family she loved. Now she felt vulnerable again; she lay in bed, stiff with tension, and told herself she was being stupid.

She wasn't a baby any longer; no one would or could take her away from her mom at this late date. Could they? Did being adopted mean you were never secure, never safe?

The old fears were too vivid in the middle of the night. Sarah wished she could call for her mother, hug her like a little kid again, feel safe in her embrace.

She didn't even have her ragged old teddy bear to hug. Where was the little stuffed lion Mark had given her? She found it in her duffel bag, then curled up and hugged it to her chest. She tried to think of good memories to push away the night terrors; she thought of picnics with her mom and dad, Thanksgiving at Nana's house, her first bicycle, the dollhouse her dad had built for her and her mom had furnished. Small bits and pieces of her life, but they added up to a strong and loving whole. Gradually, Sarah relaxed, and finally she slept again.

She woke to hear someone knocking at her door. "What?" Sarah called groggily.

"Are you ready for breakfast, Sarah?"

For a moment she thought she was at home, then the strange bedroom, the unfamiliar voice, brought everything back. She glanced at the clock on the bedside table. It was nine-thirty; she remembered the hours for breakfast.

"Yes, I'll be right there," she called, then pushed herself up.

Daylight streamed through the white curtains and made the rose-patterned wallpaper look fresh and clean. With morning, the nightmares seemed far away and much less frightening.

Sarah pulled off her sleep shirt and put her shorts and T-shirt back on, running a comb carefully through her hair. It was thinner, she was sure it was thinner. Sighing, she grabbed her purse and went out to find her breakfast.

The meal was served in a sunny dining room toward the back of the big house. Neat white tablecloths covered several small tables, and Sarah was the only one in the room. Sarah saw a plateful of soft scrambled eggs and crisp bacon, and there were light baking powder biscuits and homemade strawberry jam, with fruit juice and milk. Even her capricious appetite responded, and Sarah ate almost all of her breakfast.

"It was very good," she told her landlady when she returned.

"Thank you." The woman smiled at her. "Would you like some coffee or tea?"

"No thank you," Sarah told her. "Is there a bus that runs toward Four Points?"

The other woman shook her head. "We're not big enough to have local buses," she explained. "Most people have their own cars, you know?"

Sarah nodded, but it wasn't much help. She thought of a rental car, and when she stood up from the table, went back to the phone in the sitting room. She called information and tried several national car rental companies. But not only was the cost expensive, she'd have to go back to Nashville to find the closest rental pickup. Sarah hung up the phone, feeling depressed again.

She went back to the kitchen and found the owner of the bed and breakfast loading a dishwasher. "Does anyone in town rent cars?" she asked.

The woman frowned, thinking. "I don't really know. You could try Harding's Garage, farther down Main. He might have something, if anyone does."

"Thanks."

She might have known it was on Main Street, Sarah told herself, grinning a little at the private joke. She wasn't sure anyone here would appreciate how small this hamlet looked to her, after growing up in a big city.

She stopped in her room to put on a little makeup, trying to disguise the paleness that her disease brought with it. In a few minutes she was on her way again, walking slowly down the main avenue of town.

She passed Second Avenue, the side street that had led her to the nursing home, then continued past the sheriff's office and then Mary Anne's Tearoom, just opening for business. Sarah looked the other way; she didn't want to face Mary Anne again, not yet. Somehow, the woman had made her feel guilty for searching. She wasn't trying to cause anyone else any trouble, Sarah told herself. Surely she had the right to try to find an answer that might save her life?

She still hadn't seen the garage, and the buildings along the street were getting farther apart, with more homes now and fewer shops. Had she missed it, while her mind worked furiously on all the old questions, the old fears?

Sarah looked around; across the street she saw a grassy expanse dotted with stone markers. An old graveyard, she realized, surrounded by a time-worn stone fence. Drawn by some compulsion she couldn't put into words, Sarah crossed the street and walked through the narrow gateway.

Silence flowed all around her; she could hear a car crunch over gravel as it turned into a driveway farther up the street, but here a bee droned near a stray wildflower, and the sweet scent of honeysuckle drifted from the vine that covered part of the old wall.

Sarah looked around at the headstones and shivered; it seemed almost like an omen, reminding her of her own perilous grip on life. How long before she, too, rested in a long box and was lowered into a hole in the ground?

"Stop it," Sarah said aloud, angry at herself. It meant nothing at all; every town had a cemetery. And there was a bench just inside the gate; she could sit and rest a minute. She was tired from all the walking she'd done, as well as from the weakness that was always with her and made her knees rubbery and her shoulders ache.

Defiantly, she walked inside and lowered herself to the cold concrete bench. She sat for a few minutes and let her mind empty of thoughts and worries. In a while, feeling slightly rested, she stood up and prepared to backtrack, searching once more for the garage. She was about to walk back to the entrance when a name on a nearby headstone caught her eye.

Of course! How better to find local family names? At the very least, she could check Mary Anne's story and see if MacPhersons had lived long enough in this area to leave their mark in the local graveyard.

She spent the next hour walking slowly through the markers, checking the names on the marble and granite stones. Some of the headstones were very old, worn smooth along the edges by decades of wind and rain. Others looked newer and had plastic flowers sitting in urns or attached to the stone itself by brackets. There was one grave still mounded with fresh dirt.

Finally, at the far corner of the grassy expanse, she found what she sought. WILLIAM MACPHERSON, the headstone said. AUGUST 1, 1918–OCTOBER 10, 1980. And his wife lay by his side; she had died even earlier. If these were Ellen MacPherson's parents, she was alone, too, at least to this extent.

It gave Sarah a strange feeling to look at these graves, so peaceful, covered with neatly cut green grass. Were these people her grandparents? But they were strangers; she had never known them, and now she never would. And where was their daughter, the elusive Ellen?

Sarah stared at the quiet graves, her mind busy. If someone died, there would be an obituary. She had seen her mom reading the obituary columns in the paper at home, when one of their elderly neighbors had died. And she remembered her father's death. They listed the surviving family in those notices, and—Sarah racked her memory—they often included the hometowns of the relatives. If she could find an obituary of William MacPherson, it might bring her one step closer to

Ellen, if she was his daughter. Too many ifs, but what else did she have?

Where would she find a local paper? Sarah sighed, her legs were tired again. But she headed out of the cemetery and turned back toward town. She stopped in the small grocery store and asked about a paper.

"A local paper—you mean the county weekly?" the girl at the cash register asked.

"Yes, thank you, do you have any left?"

The cashier nodded, and Sarah paid a quarter to buy a thin newspaper and glanced at it quickly. She located the masthead and read the address, then shook her head in disappointment. The newspaper office was in Four Points. She had to find some transportation; she was too tired to keep walking all day, and this was too far to go on foot.

"Could you tell me where to find Harding's Garage?" she asked the girl before she left.

The young woman gave directions, and this time Sarah found it without any problem. The garage sat on a corner lot, behind a large soft drink sign, hardly noticeable from the main road. Its big doors faced the side street, and the sign over the doors was small. No doubt everyone here knew where it was located already, Sarah told herself.

She walked to the big open doorway and looked around. A station wagon and a pickup truck took up the two stalls. At first she thought no one was around, then a movement caught her eye. A man lay on his back under the station wagon; she could see only his legs.

"Hello?" Sarah called.

The man rolled himself backward, then stood up. He was dressed in a grease-stained coverall, but his face was clean, except for one smear across his cheek.

"Howdy," he said. He held out his hand to shake, then looked at the deep stains on his fingers and changed his mind, rubbing his hands absently on his coverall. "Mike Harding. Can I help you, young lady?"

Sarah said, "I hope so. Would you possibly have a car to rent? I don't care what kind, or if it's new or not."

He pursed his lips. "Sorry, no."

"Nothing?" Sarah asked, her tone shrill with desperation.

"Well—" He seemed to consider, looking her over thoughtfully.

"What?" Sarah asked quickly.

"I'll show you." He led the way past the station wagon to the back of the building, then stopped and waved.

Sarah stared; a small motor scooter, slightly rusty in spots, sat behind a pile of tires, prim as an old lady in a pool hall.

"It was my wife's," Mike told her. "But we got a good deal on a '68 Mustang, and I rebuilt the engine, and now she's tooling around town in that.

Do you know how to ride one? I could rent you this, say ten dollars a day?"

Sarah thought quickly. She'd ridden a friend's small motorbike a few times when she was fourteen—until her mom found out and put a quick end to the practice. The scooter couldn't be that different, surely, and it would beat walking.

"Sure," she said. "I've ridden a motorbike, anyhow."

"Can you make a deposit?" he asked her, a little doubtfully. "Since I don't know you, and all."

"I have a credit card," Sarah told him.

"That'll do," he agreed. He took an imprint of her card, checked her signature, and glanced at her driver's license. Fortunately, he didn't seem to think about checking to see if she was certified to drive motorcycles, because she wasn't.

Mike pushed the motor scooter out to the lot, and showed her how to work the controls. Sarah got on gingerly, gripping the handles almost too tightly, but after one false start, she had no trouble steering the little vehicle around the parking lot. She braked too abruptly, but with a little practice, it wouldn't be hard to drive, she thought.

"Not bad," Mike decided. "Just take it easy, okay? And here, you can borrow this as part of the deal." He walked back to the office and found her a hot pink helmet adorned with golden stars.

His wife had interesting tastes, Sarah thought fleetingly. She took the helmet and fastened it over her head, trying not to think what her mom would say about this. "Thank you," she said. "I'll probably keep it several days."

She had already told him both where she was staying in town and her home address and phone. She gunned the motor and pulled out onto the street. She drove the scooter almost too cautiously for a few blocks, then, when she was sure she could manage it, the knots in her stomach eased. Now she could head to Four Points, check the obituaries in the county newspaper, maybe find a clue to Ellen's whereabouts.

Beneath the wildly colored helmet, Sarah grinned. Now she had a chance at finding the answers she needed. She was on her way.

Chapter
Eleven

Dear Diary,

At last I have wheels. It's not a fancy car, but the motor scooter, old as it is, will get me around, and I'm so tired of walking. I had to come back to the bed and breakfast and take a nap, now I'm checking my map again, ready to head for Four Points and look for more clues to Ellen's location.

Please God, let me find her!

Sarah sighed. The brief rest had helped a little, but only a little. She needed more than sleep; she needed a bone marrow donor, and Ellen was her only chance.

She put the diary away and pushed the map into her purse, just in case. She stood up, feeling a little dizzy, then took a deep breath and waited for the room to steady; she wouldn't get sick, now, she just wouldn't. She pulled on the helmet, fastened its strap, put her purse over her shoulder, and headed for the parking lot in back of the building where she had parked the little scooter.

Starting the motor, she headed for the street. She'd already memorized the route, and she followed Main Street into the center of town, where it crossed a state road. FOUR POINTS, the sign obligingly said, 12 MILES.

With a vehicle, she felt much more in control. Sarah signaled, then turned carefully and zipped along the street. Soon, she was out of the small town and driving past green fields and thick groves of trees. A mockingbird flew past her, white feathers flashing against gray. A squirrel ran across the road, and she slowed to be certain to miss it. A road sign warned of curves, then another noted a deer crossing.

Sarah seemed very far from the busy streets of Los Angeles. She felt suddenly lonely for her mom, for Mark, for Maria and her other friends. What did she have to do with this lush green countryside? She was more accustomed to dry brown summers, where the only greenery was maintained with sprinklers and careful attention, to towering palm trees and sea gulls instead of songbirds.

Never mind. If she found what she needed, she could be home very soon. Sarah concentrated on driving, and in a few minutes she saw houses dotted along the road as another small town came into view.

Four Points looked slightly larger than Pleasant Hills, Sarah thought. There were two gas stations on the edge of town, and a bigger city hall. A discount store and supermarket shared a large parking lot and there were several churches, and a bigger school. Election signs plastered every available electric pole and dotted the smoothly mowed lawns. Where was the newspaper office?

Sarah drove slowly along the street, checking the buildings on either side. When her first check didn't reveal any sign of the building, she retraced her route, and considered turning onto one of the larger side streets. The paper's masthead hadn't had a street address, just a post office box number.

She turned into the first gas station and filled up the small tank of the scooter. When she paid for the gas, she spoke to the old man who tended the register.

"Can you tell me where the newspaper office is located?"

He pointed. "Two blocks down, then take a left on Crabapple Lane."

"Thanks." Sarah hopped back on her scooter and set out again. This time, she found the small white block office right away and parked in front, pulling off her helmet.

Inside the small building, she saw a front desk with a tidy stack of newspapers sitting on one corner, and a Chamber of Commerce plaque hanging on the wall, next to a photo of a Little League team.

Sarah looked around for an employee, and a

blond-haired girl, not much older than Sarah, came out of an inner office.

"Hi. You need to place an ad?"

"No, actually I'd like to check the obituaries from 1980," Sarah explained. "I'm—I'm doing some family research."

"Oh." The girl looked at her curiously. "A school project, or just personal?"

"Personal," Sarah answered, her voice sounding husky even to her own ears. She waited, almost holding her breath, until the girl nodded.

"We put all the old issues on microfilm years ago; the machine's a bit cranky, but if you're willing to coax it, it should work."

She led Sarah to a side office, with stacks of boxes on one side, rows of photo boxes crowding a bookshelf, side by side with several dictionaries and three volumes of an old encyclopedia. A more up-to-date computer terminal sat on the biggest desk, and the microfilm viewer was tucked into a corner. It was a bulky machine, considerably outdated.

"It's a real dinosaur," the blond girl agreed, echoing Sarah's thoughts. "But we don't have a big budget here, and it does still work. Here, I'll show you what to do."

In a few minutes Sarah had mastered the controls and sat down with the canister holding the 1980 issues of the newspaper. She started with the first of October, and scrolled carefully through several issues before she found the name she sought.

Sarah held her breath, fiddled with the controls to enlarge the print so she could read it more easily, and scanned the obituary notice quickly.

It was a relatively long entry; he must have been an important person, in this county, at least, she thought.

William Daniel MacPherson, 62, Lake Road, Pleasant Hills, died at County Hospital after a sudden illness. The funeral will be at Christ Church, Pleasant Hills, on Saturday at 2:00 with the Rev. Adam Canton officiating. Burial will be in Pleasant Hills Cemetery. Visitation will continue at Merymont Funeral Home until Friday evening, 8:00.

He was born September 1, 1918, in Louisville, Kentucky, son of Isaiah MacPherson and Martha Wilson MacPherson. He was graduated from Cincinnati Seminary, and after previous posts in Ohio and Kentucky, he had served as pastor for Christ Church for the last fifteen years. He received many honors for service to the community, including the county Man of the Year Award in 1972 and 1978. He served on the steering committee for the successful drive to build a new hospital wing at County Hospital, and worked for numerous local charities. He was chairman of the successful Fight Against Pornography Campaign in 1975 . . .

Well, Sarah thought. A big frog in a small pond; she was impressed despite herself. William MacPherson seemed to have been a very active force in his area. And a minister—that must have made it very difficult for his daughter to deal with an unplanned pregnancy. Sarah had more sympathy, suddenly, for Ellen, the preacher's daughter, suddenly confronted by undeniable evidence of behavior that her father would surely disapprove of. Had she been fearful, despairing?

Sarah glanced through the rest of the article to find the most important information, at least to her.

Survivors include a daughter, Ellen Elizabeth MacPherson Wright, Shady Valley, and a sister, Janet MacPherson O'Dowdy, Chicago, Illinois.

That was all? If his sister had children or grandchildren, they weren't listed here, and surely they would have been. And if Janet was still alive today, she was likely too old to be considered as a donor. That led right back to Ellen, again. She also hadn't had any children listed in 1980, but she was married, and she might have by now.

At least Sarah had a little more information. Now she had Ellen's married name and a town. She wrote down the information with shaking fingers, even though she knew she wouldn't forget it, and turned off the machine.

"Thank you," she called to the girl who had

helped her, who was now working at a computer terminal in the next office.

"Hope you found what you needed," the blond girl answered.

"I think so," Sarah told her.

Now she wanted to check her map again. Excitement coursed through her like a life-giving transfusion of hope. For a few minutes she could forget her constant fatigue, the depression and worry that pulled her down. She was a little closer to finding Ellen.

The success, limited as it was, had spurred her uncertain appetite. Maybe in this town she could find something besides fast food; the hospital nutritionist wouldn't have approved of all the hamburgers and fries she'd been eating. Vegetables sounded good.

Sarah went back to her rented scooter, thankful that she didn't have to walk, and cruised along the street until she found a small café. She parked again, pulled off the bright helmet, and tried to fluff up her hair. Then, with the helmet under one arm, she went inside and sat down at a narrow booth.

A thin waitress in a pink dress brought her a tired-looking menu. Sarah glanced through the choices. "What's the daily special?"

The waitress smacked her gum. "Meat loaf and fresh green beans, fresh tomatoes, coleslaw, roll or corn muffin."

Sarah nodded. "I'll try it, with the muffin, and a glass of milk, please."

While she waited for her meal, Sarah pulled the map of Tennessee out of her purse. Shady Valley wasn't listed on the index; perhaps it was another hamlet and too small to be included.

She was still scanning the map when the waitress returned with a full plate. Sarah reluctantly put the colored sheet aside and picked up her fork. The meat loaf was so-so, she discovered, but the vegetables, despite being more highly seasoned than she was accustomed to, were indeed fresh and good. The tomatoes tasted as if they'd just come off the vine, smooth textured and sweet with flavor. The green beans were good, too, although not as crunchy as when her mom fixed them. Sarah ate a good portion of her vegetables and half the muffin, then drank almost all her milk. Her mom would approve.

Then Sarah went back to her map. She was still studying it, examining the small print trying to find the name she sought, when the waitress returned.

"Want any dessert? We got apple pie."

"No thanks," Sarah answered absently. Then she looked up over the map. "Do you happen to know where Shady Valley is?"

"Shady Valley, sure. It's just outside of town." The waitress picked up the plate Sarah had pushed back and piled the silverware on top.

"You mean it's not another town?" Sarah was confused for a moment.

The waitress chuckled. "Just 'cause it's got a fancy name? No, it's a big farm, that's all. Off Route 12; you'll see a sign. Lots of excitement out there this week."

She headed back to the kitchen before Sarah could ask more and disappeared from view. Annoyed, Sarah thought of the newspaper editor who had assumed that everyone knew where Shady Valley was; maybe around here, they did.

But that meant Ellen might be listed in the local phone book, if she hadn't moved since the obituary notice was printed.

Sarah paid her bill, then went outside and looked around. There at the corner, next to the ice cream shop, she saw a public phone. Sarah walked across, but found no phone book in the slot.

Frustrated, she walked back inside the café and spoke to the cashier, a middle-aged man who sat on a stool behind the cash register, now reading the sports pages.

"Do you have a phone book I could see, please?"

"Public phone outside," he murmured, not looking up.

"I know that, but there's no phone book attached," Sarah said, trying to keep the sharpness out of her tone. "I'd just like to see the phone book."

"Sure." He put down his newspaper long enough to reach beneath the counter and find another small green telephone book.

Sarah took it eagerly, then leaned on the counter and flipped through the pages.

Wright—she found four Wrights listed, but one was James Wright, Shady Valley Farms.

And there was the phone number. Sarah drew in her breath sharply.

The man behind the cash register looked up in surprise, and Sarah tried to look natural, tried not to show the nervous anticipation that suddenly made her tense all over.

She could just walk out and call her birth mother! After all this time, Sarah had the number; she knew where to find her.

She wrote the number quickly on the edge of her map, then returned the telephone directory to the cashier with a polite "Thank you."

Then she walked outside, wanting to be alone, away from watching eyes. She felt almost light-headed. She had the number!

Maybe this wasn't the right way, to just call up out of the blue. What if she scared Ellen, shocked her.

But Sarah didn't know another way to do it, didn't know a family friend to break the news gently, a middle party who could smooth the way for her. And she couldn't waste any more time.

She fished a quarter out of her purse, then squared her shoulders and marched to the telephone. She dialed the number, then waited anxiously for the ring.

Instead she got a busy signal.

Sarah whistled sharply through her teeth, just like her dad had taught her when she was seven. What a terrible letdown; she had been braced to hear a woman's voice, to wonder if this was Ellen, her birth mother, at long last.

What was she going to say to her, anyhow? Sarah couldn't seem to get her mind to work. She pressed down the button, put the quarter back into the slot, and dialed again. The beep-beep-beep came once more; the line was still busy.

Sarah was ready to kick the metal post that supported the pay phone. She hung up the receiver and forced herself to wait five minutes, watching an occasional car or pickup truck drive past her, ignoring a boy's curious stare, watching a brown, untidy dog trot past, sniffing at every doorway and lamppost and fire hydrant.

At last, she dialed again. This time the phone rang. Sarah waited, almost unable to breathe.

"Hello, Wright residence."

Her mouth had gone very dry; it seemed to be stuffed with cotton. Sarah struggled to swallow, to speak. "I—I want to speak to Ellen MacPherson Wright, please."

"This is she."

"I think—I think you may be my mother," Sarah blurted. The blood pounded in her ears, and she held the phone so tightly that her knuckles were white.

There was a long silence. "What did you say?" The woman's tone was chilly, distant.

Whatever Sarah had hoped for, it wasn't this.

"I mean, I think maybe I'm the baby you gave up for adoption." Sarah tried to be plainer, tried to keep her voice from shaking.

"You must have the wrong number," the woman said, very low. The phone clicked in Sarah's ear, and the connection died.

Chapter
Twelve

Dear Maria,

I'm writing you this postcard because I don't know what to do. I thought I had found my birth mother, but when I tried to call, she hung up on me. I don't know if I've got the wrong person after all, or she just doesn't want to talk to me. If my life didn't depend on it, I wouldn't care so much. But it does.

Sarah tucked the postcard in her purse. She'd bought it from the small shop next to the café; she'd mail it later. Maybe what she had written to Maria wasn't true, completely; maybe she would still care. Okay, she didn't expect Ellen to act like a mother; Sarah already had a mother. But to be rejected so abruptly—it hurt. Wasn't Ellen curious to see how Sarah had turned out, what kind of person she was?

How could she not care, even a little, about the baby she'd given up?

Sarah walked back to the phone and dialed the number again. But this time the busy signal beeped at her. She waited five minutes, then dialed twice more, but each time all she heard was the beep-beep-beep. Was the phone busy, or had Ellen taken it off the hook? Was she avoiding Sarah on purpose? Why, because she knew Sarah's accusation was true, or did she simply think Sarah was a prank caller?

Maybe Sarah didn't have the right person; maybe Ellen wasn't the woman who'd given birth to her. But there was the photo in the yearbook, that touch of familiarity. Sarah didn't believe she was mistaken.

Maybe Ellen thought Sarah would demand money or want something else from her. Maybe she thought she'd be angry, yell at her for giving her up.

Sarah hadn't explained very well; she shouldn't have just blurted it out like she did. She should have built up to the news, been more tactful, diplomatic.

But she hadn't. And what could she do, now?

Discouragement brought back all her fatigue and weakness, redoubled. Sarah needed to sit down. She looked around and saw a city bench across the street, in front of the county courthouse. The big old brick building was set in the center of a square, and grass and flower beds surrounded it. Sarah walked across the street and sat heavily down onto the bench. Farther down, another bench held two elderly men, playing checkers. They glanced up at her, expressions curious.

Sarah felt conspicuous. She looked away from their gaze and pulled the folded newspaper she'd bought earlier out of her purse. She hadn't really read it before, just searched for the address. Now as she glanced over the columns of small print, her eye caught a familiar name. She sat up straighter, scanning the notice with growing excitement.

Under "What's Happening This Week," the top listing read:

Election rally for state representative hopeful James Wright will be held Saturday afternoon at 2:00 at Shady Valley Farms. All supporters are cordially invited for free barbecue and iced tea.

Today! And it was almost two right now. Sarah drew a deep breath. With all the people who would be there, surely they wouldn't notice one extra teenager. She might be able to get a look at Ellen, maybe even speak to her.

With new hope, her fatigue seemed to lift. Sarah stood up and almost ran across the quiet street toward her parked scooter. She pulled the helmet back on and gunned the motor.

She took only one wrong turn, and in less than half an hour she had discovered the big wooden sign that said Shady Valley. She turned off the two-lane highway and drove past the open gate. Cars and vans and pickup trucks were parked all along the long drive, and Sarah saw several vans marked with television logos. The campaign was important local news, apparently.

She parked the scooter in a small space between two cars, and walked toward the big old farmhouse she could see at the end of the drive. Everywhere, she saw WRIGHT FOR STATE REPRESENTATIVE signs. She had been seeing the red and white signs ever since she had gotten off the bus, but hadn't realized they would have any connection to her. Ellen's husband was running for state office, a politician, yet.

Sarah shook her head at the irony of it—the mystery woman she had been searching so hard for had probably been in every local newspaper and TV news show—but it would have done Sarah little good, until she found the right name. A considerable crowd of people surrounded the wide porch and filled the green lawn. There were picnic tables and folding chairs, lots of balloons and campaign posters. All around, people talked and laughed; the crowd flowed across the lawn and made it hard to tell where the center of the rally was. Where was Ellen?

Sarah walked slowly through the rear of the crowd, not wanting to draw attention to herself.

A smiling woman with a tray offered her a tall paper cup of iced tea. Sarah's mouth was dry again from tension; she accepted the cup, nodding her thanks, and sipped. The liquid eased the dryness in her throat. It was heavily sweetened, but then, she probably needed all the energy she could manage, Sarah thought wryly.

Someone at the front of the crowd was calling for quiet; Sarah found an empty folding chair and sank down onto it. A couple of camera crews shifted their position, and Sarah pulled her chair to the side to see more clearly. The talking gradually died, and now she could see a man standing on a small platform at the front. He had a portable microphone, and with a lot of pomp, he introduced the local favorite, "Our choice for state representative, James Wright."

Applause and a few cheers, then Wright himself stepped up to the mike. Sarah leaned sideways to see around a tall man with a baseball cap. Wright was of medium height, broad-framed, with a sun-reddened, smiling face and a receding hairline. He looked prosperous and confident.

"Thank you for coming today, my friends. With support like this, I have no doubt that I will be the next state representative." He paused for another wave of applause, then continued. "I'm going to Nashville to fight for family values, to fight against complacency and arrogance . . ."

Sarah stopped listening to his words and scanned the people clustered around him, searching for the woman who was Ellen MacPherson Wright. Surely the candidate's wife would be here? Why couldn't she find her?

How much had Ellen changed since that faded high school photo had been taken? Could she be the plump middle-aged woman standing toward the side, with short curly hair? Sarah struggled to see a resemblance, but couldn't be sure. And there, next to her, a thinner, taller woman with brown hair and sunglasses—perhaps the glasses obscured the face Sarah was searching for.

Sarah strained to remember the face in the yearbook; she wished belatedly that she'd had the chance to make a photocopy of it. But the image had been burned into her brain; she could still see the youthful features, the old-fashioned hairstyle. Sarah looked around the crowd, growing more anxious as she failed to spot the woman she sought.

Then, at last, Wright finished his speech. There was applause. Sarah clapped politely with the rest, not wanting to look conspicuous. Then some of the reporters called out questions, and Wright answered quickly and smoothly, without stopping to consider. And as a cameraman with a portable video camera moved a little closer to focus in on his face, Sarah saw a woman at the side who had been hidden from her view.

It was Ellen! It had to be; Sarah recognized the nose and the set of the eyes, the arch of the dark brows. And more—the yearbook photo had been in black and white—Ellen had auburn hair!

Sarah felt weak; she was glad she was sitting down. She touched her own red-brown hair, cut short and layered to hide its thinning. Red hair;

Ellen had red hair. Surely, this was the right woman.

Sarah stared at her, afraid to go closer, afraid that Ellen would see her amid the crowd and reject her again. Would Ellen even recognize Sarah? But the ghost of a resemblance was there, and it might tell her too much. Sarah didn't want to be cut off so abruptly again, not until she had the chance to plead her case more fully. Did Ellen look tense, her eyes worried above the wide smile she flashed for the crowd? Sarah couldn't be sure.

"Let's have a family picture," one of the photographers called, and Ellen smiled and moved forward, motioning to someone else outside of Sarah's vantage point.

Ellen had children! Sarah held her breath while the family arranged itself on the platform, smiling obligingly for the still cameras and video units. A tall boy with short reddish hair and freckles who looked thirteen or fourteen, another boy about ten, and a little girl who might have been six or eight.

Three children—Sarah had three half brothers and sisters—it was an incredible thought. She watched the family group as Ellen put one arm around her youngest child, the little girl with the strawberry-blond hair and spotless blue dress trimmed with white lace. The two boys were neatly dressed in pale blue shirts and dark trousers, all immaculately groomed and smiling—a picture-perfect family, all set for cameras and TV images.

She might have been part of that, if Ellen had not given her up for adoption. Sarah might have grown up in the big white house behind them, part of a large, noisy family, instead of as an only child.

What would it have been like to have little brothers to torment her, a little sister to tag along after her? Would she have read bedtime stories to them, or soothed a scratched knee with hugs and Band-Aids? Would they have loved her, cried for her when they were hurt, come to her for help with homework or for solace when they quarreled with friends?

It was like glimpsing another world. For just a moment, Sarah heard echoes of children laughing, of noisy family gatherings, and she imagined belonging here, in surroundings that seemed so alien. She felt a sharp ache inside her, for having missed all that.

Then the vision faded, and she shook her head. She would never wish to give up the parents she had, the friends she had grown up with, every piece of her childhood that had helped make her what she was today. Whatever Ellen and the unknown man who had fathered her had contributed, it was little compared to the years of love and care and understanding she had received from her mom and dad.

Sarah took a deep breath, feeling her own world settle back into place. It was like the sense of peace that came just after an earthquake, when the shaking had stopped, and the solidity of the ground beneath you seemed dependable once more. She was Sarah Davenport, and she had no wish to be anyone else.

The photographers had finally lowered their cameras and were packing equipment away. The crowd was slowly dispersing, and James Wright and his wife were talking to scattered groups of people, shaking hands, smiling, campaigning.

Sarah walked around the edge of the group, still aware that she didn't want to be noticed too soon. She had to catch Ellen Wright almost alone, to say something in private, but not wait too late until Ellen retreated to the house, where Sarah couldn't go without attracting attention.

Getting arrested for trespassing would hardly be the best way to start out with her birth mother, after a seventeen-year absence, she thought, trying to make a joke of it.

But she couldn't laugh, because it mattered too much. With patience that was painful to maintain, she sipped her tea and watched from the corner of her eye as Ellen spoke to one person after another; there was always someone else waiting in line to speak to her. And what Sarah had to say, she couldn't say in front of a curious audience.

The minutes dragged, and Sarah waited tensely, gripping her paper cup so tightly that it finally crumpled, and she had to shake the drops of iced tea off her hand. She found a trash barrel to toss it into and wiped her damp, sticky hands on a tissue.

But at last, the crowd was thinning noticeably,

and Ellen shook one more hand, glanced toward her husband, who was still talking to a small group, then turned back toward the house. All three children had disappeared inside right after the picture taking had ended.

If she didn't catch her now, Sarah would lose her chance. She hurried forward, almost running, so that she could catch up with Ellen before she reached the front porch.

Ellen must have heard the sound of footsteps behind her, because she glanced over her shoulder. Her expression was wary, the skin tight around her eyes, and her lips pressed thinly together.

Would she hurry away? No, to Sarah's relief, Ellen turned and faced her squarely. "Yes? If you want to volunteer to help the campaign, please stop by the campaign headquarters in town. It was nice of you to come today."

It was a dismissal, but Sarah wouldn't be put off so easily.

"It's not about the campaign," she said. "I called you—I really need to speak to you."

Ellen paled, and she took a step backward. "I can't—you have the wrong person. You're mistaken, I'm sorry. It isn't me you want."

Sarah looked her in the eye. "Can you really look at me and say that?" she asked, her tone level. Standing this close, the likeness was more pronounced, the tilt of the brow, the strong cheekbones, the shape of the lower lip. And of course, the red hair.

Ellen stared at Sarah as if she were some newly discovered poisonous insect; she looked shaken, even scared.

"I don't—I can't talk about this; I'm sorry."

"I'm going to die," Sarah said. She hated to use emotional blackmail, but if this woman wouldn't even speak to her, what else could she do but be blunt. "Don't you even care?"

Silence. Ellen's eyes widened. "Are you telling the truth? You're so young, I mean, what—"

Another woman was approaching. "Ellen, do you need help cleaning up? I can stay if you like."

"Thank you, Caroline, I'll be right with you. Why don't you wait inside for me and rest just a minute, then we'll start clearing away." The automatic smile flashed, but underneath, Sarah could still see the tension that left Ellen's eyes wide and frightened.

"I can't talk here," she said quickly, her voice low as the other woman walked toward the porch.

"Then where?" Sarah persisted.

Ellen waved her hand as if to drive away a pesky gnat. The effort it took for her to think was obvious. "Tomorrow morning is church. Then there's a luncheon with the Garden Club. Then I was going to stop by the campaign headquarters," she said. "But I'll meet you, oh, let me think. Are you staying in Four Points?"

Sarah shook her head. "At the bed and breakfast in Pleasant Hills."

Ellen made up her mind. "I'll meet you at two

o'clock in the Pleasant Hills graveyard. There's a bench back under the trees, not the one at the front. Please don't say anything to anyone else."

"I won't," Sarah answered quickly, stung that Ellen might think she was a troublemaker. "If I didn't have a good reason, I wouldn't—"

"Tomorrow," Ellen said quickly. Two other people were approaching them, and Ellen said more loudly, "Thank you for coming; we appreciate everyone's support."

Then she turned to the couple behind Sarah, smiling once more, and Sarah had to turn away.

She walked slowly back down the drive to her scooter, no longer crowded among the parked cars, as most of the vehicles had already pulled away.

Would Ellen come, as she had promised? What would she say to Sarah's plea?

Chapter

Thirteen

Dear Maria,

She's going to come and see me, she says. I
hope she keeps her word. Does she believe that
my life depends on it? Think about me, Maria,
and light a candle for me. I need all the help I
can get.

Sarah sat on the parked motor scooter and
scribbled onto the bottom of the card. The postcard was almost full; Sarah had to write the words
in a tiny script. But she wanted so badly to talk to
someone, anyone who cared. She felt so alone out
here in a strange state, without her mom and her
friends, without Mark to hold her hand and put his
arms around her.

Maybe she just wanted to remember that there
were people who did love her, who valued her,
who didn't try to ignore her and pretend she didn't
exist.

Sarah lifted her chin, and some of her hurt inside turned to anger. She looked back up the driveway to the big white house at the end of the lane. She wasn't trying to embarrass Ellen; she wasn't going to run to the local gossip columnist, whoever that might be. Was it the election campaign? How important could a race for a lousy state post be, for crying out loud?

She kicked at a rock in the drive, wanting to lash out at someone, anyone. Yet, she was also curiously reluctant to leave. Her birth mother was so close, inside the closed door of the farmhouse, yet so far. This was where the answers lay, if Ellen would only share them with her.

At least Sarah had gotten a good look at her birth mother; she had no more doubts in her mind about Ellen's identity. What about her birth father —could he be that complacent small-time politician who had spoken so confidently on the platform?

Surely not; if that were the man, why wouldn't he and Ellen have married? Or was there some family reason they had to wait? Ellen must have married him not too long after Sarah had been born and given up for adoption, Sarah thought, because the oldest boy looked only a few years younger than Sarah herself.

But if James Wright wasn't her birth father, who was? Her other birth parent would be another potential donor, and if he had children, there could be even more. How could she find out? Would her father be listed on her original birth certificate, if she could find it? Her adopted parents had never been told her family background; it was a closed adoption, without the names of the baby's parents being shared.

Sighing, Sarah pulled on the helmet and started the little scooter. No point in hanging around here any longer, like some encyclopedia salesman who had been turned away from the door. Most of the other guests had already left. She pulled into the driveway and turned back toward the highway.

"Look out!"

At the shout, she twisted the handles of the scooter abruptly, almost overturning it as she steered it to the side of the driveway. A large green tractor barreled down the lane, almost clipping her smaller vehicle.

She fought to maintain her balance, her heart in her throat. But in a moment she had righted the too sharp angle of the scooter. She drew a deep breath of relief, finally able to glare at the big tractor that had almost run her down. Who was driving?

It was the oldest red-haired boy who looked back over his shoulder at her, frowning. He'd changed from his dress-up clothes; now he wore cutoff jeans and had a ball cap pulled low over his eyes.

Don't glare at me; it wasn't my fault, Sarah wanted to yell after him. Why was he driving such a big machine, anyhow, at his age, and much too fast?

She had to restart the scooter's engine, then she followed the tractor slowly, after checking up and down the driveway for more hazards. When she reached the entrance to the highway, Sarah saw that the tractor had traveled along the public road for a few dozen yards, and was now turning into a field.

The boy didn't look at her again, and Sarah pointed her motor scooter back toward town. She'd stop in Four Points again on the way back to her lodging. It seemed to be the county seat; surely they would have birth records in the courthouse. It wouldn't hurt to check for a birth certificate; it was an obvious clue, and she couldn't afford to pass up any hope, no matter how meager.

She had so much to think about that the fifteen-minute drive back to town went swiftly, and she hardly noticed the fields around her with their flitting birds until a lone hawk sitting high in a tree suddenly took wing, zooming down to catch its dinner.

Sarah gasped, watching the small bird falter, then pull away from the diving predator, apparently eluding the grip of the cruel talons. But one wing seemed to move awkwardly as it flew into a bush, out of reach. Frustrated, the hawk circled again, waiting for the bird to reemerge.

Sarah slowed the scooter and pulled it to a stop on the side of the road. The little bird had been wounded; would it escape the hawk? She felt tears on her cheeks and shook her head; this was silly.

But she felt such a sympathy for the wounded creature that she shouted at the hawk. "Leave it alone!"

The bigger bird, startled by the noise, veered away.

Sarah wiped her cheeks, sighing. Life and death were all around her. Small creatures died every day; why should this be any different? But she wanted the bird to live; she wanted to live. She refused to give up.

She pulled back onto the road and increased her speed. The sun was warm against her back, and the wind brushed her short hair. She felt very tired, but she couldn't waste the rest of the afternoon. Her fatigue was growing; how much longer would she be able to keep up this search? Sarah thought wistfully of catching the bus back to Nashville, of flying home and having her mom's arms around her, of seeing Mark and having Maria come by to tell her the latest news from school. Normal life, that's all she wanted, and life itself, most of all.

When she drove back into the quiet town, she parked her scooter along the square and dug out a nickel to slip into the old-fashioned parking meter. Then she walked into the big brick courthouse with its wide, dusty halls and glass-paned doors.

After a couple of false turns and some polite questions, she found the right office.

"May I help you?" the gray-haired lady behind the desk asked, peering at her through narrow glasses.

"Umm, I'm doing some research on births and deaths," Sarah told her, trying to keep her voice steady. "It's for a school report."

The woman nodded, apparently without suspicion. "We have all the county records on computer, now," she explained. "But I can let you check the statistics if you don't take too long. Do you know how to use a computer?"

Sarah nodded quickly, her pulse jumping again.

The woman led her to a gray computer terminal and punched in the codes for the files. She showed Sarah how to find the birth and death certificates, and went back to her desk.

Sarah felt tense with anticipation. She punched in her birthday, then hit the enter key. She waited while the computer hummed, then brought up the solitary entry.

There was one birth listed on that day! Sarah punched the keys to bring up the birth certificate itself, holding her breath.

It was a boy, born to Marion and David Wallace.

Sarah exhaled slowly; another dead end. Either her mom had been told the wrong birth date, or Sarah hadn't been born in this county at all.

She stared at the gray screen, thinking hard. If Ellen had wanted to keep her pregnancy a secret, she would have gone somewhere else for the birth of her baby, but where?

There was no way for Sarah to guess, not without a great deal more information about Ellen and her family.

"Are you finished with the computer, dear?" the woman asked from the next desk.

"Yes, I think so," Sarah said. "Thank you for your help."

She pushed her purse strap back over her shoulder and walked slowly out of the courthouse.

All she came up with were blanks. The answers to all her questions lay with Ellen; would she share any or all of the information? Would she admit to giving up a child; would she agree that her baby had grown up to become Sarah? And even more important, would she agree that she and her children would be tested, in case any one of them might be a compatible donor?

Sarah walked across to the café and ordered a thick bowl of vegetable soup. She ate as much as she could, then returned to the scooter and headed back to Pleasant Valley and the bed and breakfast.

When she walked into the old house, she could hear people talking in the front room, more guests, maybe. But she didn't feel at all sociable, and her shoulders were sagging with exhaustion. She went straight to her own room, unlocked the door, and went in, closing it behind her. She dropped down on the bed, too tired to move.

Tomorrow she would find out if Ellen was willing to help her. If she said yes, it could be a new beginning for Sarah, if any of her birth family tested as compatible donors, if the transplant was a success, if she survived all the possible side effects and complications. But she would have a chance. If Ellen said no, there would be no hope at all.

It was too much to think about. Sarah tried to put it all out of her mind. She had pushed herself too far today; she could feel the flush of fever in her face, and her arms and legs trembled with weakness. Then she remembered that she'd promised to call her mom back, and almost groaned at the thought of having to get up again. She was too tired. But her mom would worry if she didn't call.

Wearily, she pushed herself up, picked up her purse, and walked quietly back to the front sitting room. To her relief, it was empty now, and she could sit down by the phone and dial.

When she'd punched in all the right codes, she heard the ringing on the other end, then her mother's familiar voice.

"Hello?"

For a moment Sarah felt tears shut her throat; she had to swallow hard before she could answer. She was glad now she'd made the effort to call; she needed to hear her mom's voice.

"It's me, Mom. Sarah."

"Sweetheart, how are you? You sound tired? Are you ill?" Her mother sounded anxious, and Sarah could picture her worried frown. "I still think I should fly out. Nana's growing stronger, and her outlook is good. I could be in Nashville in a few hours."

"No, Mom." Sarah took a deep breath and tried to sound more confident. "I am tired, but I'm okay. I was able to speak to Ellen; she agreed to come and talk to me tomorrow afternoon."

"I'm glad, Sarah. I hope it all goes well, and she's willing to be tested as a donor. But I'm worried about your condition. Are you sure you don't want me to come?"

"No, please. I—I think I need to do this myself."

There was silence on the line; had she hurt her mother? Could her mom understand how mixed up her feelings were about this woman who had given birth to her, how she needed to speak to her alone? Sarah bit her lip, then said slowly, "Mom?"

"Yes?"

"You're always my mother first; you know that, don't you? I'll never feel for anyone else the way I feel about you, the way I love you."

This time she heard the huskiness in her mother's voice. "Thank you, Sweetheart. That means a lot. I just want you to have your chance to get well. That's the most important thing, now, wherever this leads."

They talked a few minutes more, and Sarah tried her best to sound reassuring. Next she spoke briefly to her grandmother, who was still gaining strength. When Sarah hung up, she felt better.

On impulse, she dialed Mark's number. He answered after only two rings.

"Hi, it's your Tennessee girlfriend," she said, trying to be flip.

"Are you okay, Sarah?"

"I'm still alive," she said. "Still walking around."

"Not funny," Mark told her.

"I didn't think it was." She had sobered, too. "Mark, I've seen my birth mother, her house, her other children, and it gives me the funniest feeling. What would I have been like if I'd been raised by another family, in another place? Maybe I'd be a whole different person. It makes me wonder who I really am."

She stopped; she didn't know how to explain the moments of fear, this strange idea that she could be fading away, changing into some other person entirely.

But he didn't belittle her inner turmoil. "I know who you are," he said, his voice steady. "You're the girl who thinks my jokes are funny, the girl who always stops to help someone who's lost, the girl who's not afraid to have the right answers in math class. You never make fun of other people, and you don't run away when you're afraid. You're stubborn and sweet and funny and brave. I know you, Sarah Davenport, so don't worry. I won't let you forget who you are, if those Tennessee people mess up your mind."

She didn't know whether to laugh or cry. "Thanks. I miss you," she said very quietly.

"I miss you, too. Come home soon, Sarah."

"I hope I can," she agreed. When she hung up the phone, she walked back to her bedroom and locked the door. She walked into the bathroom for a glass of water and gulped down her antibiotic pill and some Tylenol for the fever. Then she pulled off her clothes, too weary to even wash her face, pulled the shades on the fading sunlight, and crawled into bed.

Tomorrow would tell whether she lived or died. Sleep tonight would surely be impossible. But she shut her eyes, and eventually exhaustion overcame her, and she slept.

Chapter
Fourteen

Dear Diary,

This is the day when I finally get to talk to the woman who gave birth to me. Mother doesn't seem the right word to call her; it seems unfair to my mom. My mom was the one who walked the floor with me when I had colic and screamed for hours, who took me to ballet lessons and soccer practice and sat in the front row at all the school programs so Dad could get enough pictures, who cried when they told us I had cancer, who sat up with me when I threw up every day and every night from the chemo. Margaret Davenport is my mother, but what do I call Ellen; what do I say to her?

More important, what is she going to say to me? Does she feel any bond, any obligation to me? Does she care if I live or die?

Today, I'll find out.

Sarah shut her diary and put it back in her duffel bag. She pulled on some clothes and walked down to the sunny dining room. She sat down at one of the tables, nodded politely to a gray-haired couple who sat at another small table, and tried to eat her breakfast.

But her throat seemed to close up; she couldn't swallow the fluffy eggs and light crumbly biscuits. Even though Sarah knew that she needed the nourishment, her stomach wouldn't allow it, not today, when everything hung in the balance.

Sarah gave up, putting down her fork and pushing back the plate. She went back to her bedroom, took a quick shower, and found a clean T-shirt to put on with her denim shorts. How would she pass the time until two o'clock?

She lay back down across her bed and tried to rest; the weariness that was always with her seemed worse this morning. Was her illness advancing? If she became too ill, she wouldn't even be able to have the bone marrow transplant. Too many worries, too many fears. Sarah was so tired of it all. She shut her eyes and tried to push away all the thoughts that whirled around and around inside her mind. She must have dozed, because she woke to a light knock at the door.

"Can I clean the room, now, dear?"

Sarah sat up, feeling groggy. "Sure," she said, glancing at the clock on the bedside table. 12:14, the digital display said. "I was just leaving."

She opened the door and let in the landlady, who pulled an ancient vacuum cleaner behind her and carried a plastic tray with cleaning supplies.

"Lovely day outside," she said.

Sarah nodded. Maybe it was. If Ellen turned her down, blue skies wouldn't help much.

She picked up the helmet and her purse and went to the parking lot in back. She started the engine on the scooter and headed toward the heart of the little town. Passing the tearoom, Sarah slowed the scooter, parking it in an empty parking place.

She walked slowly into the small dining room, glancing around at the tables dotted with Sunday diners, and smelling the fragrant aroma of fresh baking. It made her mouth water and reminded her of the emptiness inside her. But her stomach was still too knotted with nervousness to allow her to eat. Maybe later, when she knew what the results of her talk with Ellen would be.

This time it was Mary Anne herself who came to wait on her. She tensed when she recognized Sarah, her welcoming smile fading, her expression blank, almost suspicious.

"Could I have a raisin scone to go, please?" Sarah asked, peering into the glass case of pastries.

The woman seemed to relax; she took a sheet of tissue paper and picked up the scone, dropping it into a small paper bag.

"That'll be a dollar and fifty-five cents," she said.

Sarah opened her purse and dug out the money. She handed it to Mary Anne, who opened the old cash register with a ding.

"Why did you lie to me?" Sarah asked quietly.

Mary Ann dropped one of the coins; it rolled away and disappeared under one of the tables, but neither of them bent to retrieve it.

"What do you mean?"

"You said you hadn't talked to Ellen since high school; she's living outside the next town, not twenty miles from here."

Her round face flushing, Mary Anne looked away from Sarah's accusing stare. "I didn't lie. I haven't seen her, not to talk to. We were best friends once, but we sort of lost touch. She keeps to herself, mostly; I've only seen her in a crowd, whenever her husband's making one of his speeches. She never comes back to the reunions at the school, or goes out with her old friends."

"Do you remember who she was dating back then?" Sarah asked.

Mary Anne stared at her. "Come into the kitchen," she said. "I have to check the oven."

Sarah followed her into the long, narrow kitchen. Mary Anne turned to frown at her again, once they were out of sight of the other diners, and put her hands on her wide hips.

"Why should I tell you that?"

"Because no matter what you believe, I'm not trying to hurt her," Sarah said. "But there are things I need to know, things I think I have a right to know."

They stared at each other, but Mary Anne was the first to lower her gaze. "I don't know; she didn't date anybody much. You'd have to know her father to understand."

"What about him?" Sarah asked.

"He was the minister of the biggest church in town, everybody knew them. She had nice clothes; she always had to be sort of perfect, you know. She couldn't wear her sweaters too tight or her skirts too short. It was that kind of family. She had nicer outfits than me, but I felt sorry for her, sometimes." Mary Anne picked up a knife and dipped it into a bowl of frosting. The cake layers sat on a round cake plate; she brushed away the crumbs, then spread the frosting smoothly across the top.

Sarah watched Mary Anne's careful motions, but it was Ellen's faded high school photo that she saw in her mind's eye.

"She left school in the middle of her junior year; she told me she was pregnant, but she wouldn't say any more. Her folks let out that she had scarlet fever. She went away for a while, came back the next fall, and finished her senior year, but she was real quiet. I always thought she'd go to college, but she got married instead. James Earl was older, already working on his family's farm, and he was real taken with her. They've been happy enough, I guess; hard for anyone else to tell, isn't it?"

Mary Anne gave one more swirl to the cake, then looked up. "That's all I know."

"Thank you," Sarah said softly. "She's coming to see me this afternoon. Maybe you've helped me avoid saying the wrong things."

She walked back out and drove the scooter on to the graveyard; it was only a few blocks farther on, but she was saving her energy as much as she could. Sarah found the bench at the back of the cemetery and sat down to wait.

It was very quiet in the old graveyard. Leaves rustled lightly in the breeze, and a bird chattered high in a treetop. The grass had been cut recently; occasional damp clumps marked the passage of the lawn mower, and she could smell the lingering scent of cut grass. Sarah looked over the time-worn stones and wondered how many secrets were buried here, old scandals, petty embarrassments. But the silence of the dead made everything else look small by comparison. Now, if she could only convince Ellen to see it the same way . . .

Sarah glanced at her watch. It was almost two; would Ellen come, or had the appointment only been a ploy to get Sarah away from the farm?

Despite her lack of energy, nervousness made it impossible for Sarah to sit still. She stood up and walked restlessly up and down.

The grave of Ellen's parents was not far from the bench; perhaps that was why Ellen had remembered its location. Sarah walked across to the double headstone and looked at it one more time. It was neatly kept, but unadorned. Perhaps Ellen didn't care for plastic flowers, or perhaps it was something else.

Sarah looked at her watch again. Five past two. What if Ellen didn't come, what would she do next? Now that Ellen was on her guard, how would Sarah get close enough to speak to her again? And how long could she stay here before her money ran out or her health deteriorated. Had this been a wild goose chase after all, the futile hope of a dying patient grasping at any chance?

The crunch of footsteps on the gravel walk made Sarah raise her head. She tensed, then hurried to meet the woman who walked slowly toward her.

Sarah stopped a few feet away, not sure how to greet her. Ellen stood very straight, her neat navy-blue suit jacket buttoned up to her chin, her hair sprayed so stiffly into place that not even the breeze that tossed the leaves on the trees could move it. Ellen stared at her daughter, and her expression was closed and hostile.

Sarah swallowed hard. What had she done to warrant this kind of aloofness, even resentment? Just because she had searched for her birth parents? She had to say something. "Thank you for coming," she murmured.

Ellen nodded, her expression still chilly. "You don't look sick. Why did you say you were dying?"

What irony—if she could feel the weakness inside of Sarah that constantly drained her strength, the woman wouldn't doubt her. Sarah's knees felt wobbly. She walked back to the bench and sat down heavily. "Because I am."

Ellen's eyes widened, but her stare was still suspicious. "Why?"

"I have leukemia."

There was a long silence as the word hung in the air between them, then Ellen took two steps and sat down, too, at the far end of the bench, leaving as much distance between them as possible.

Sarah watched her perch on the far end, hurt despite herself. You needn't worry, she wanted to say. If my life didn't depend on it, I wouldn't be here. But she couldn't make the woman angry, too much was at stake, and Sarah was the supplicant. It was Ellen who had all the power.

"But I thought—" Ellen cleared her throat; she avoided meeting Sarah's eyes. "I thought that was not as—that the treatment had improved, and most of the children with leukemia lived, not like it was years ago."

"They have improved the treatments, and most of the young patients do survive, but not all. I seem to be in the last category," Sarah said, taking refuge in black humor. She didn't want to show her fear in front of this unsympathetic woman with her cold eyes. "This is my third remission; the chemotherapy isn't working anymore."

"What—what do you want? Do you need money?" Ellen's eyes had narrowed.

Sarah flushed in embarrassment. Is that all Ellen could think of? And she still looked suspicious, as if not quite believing Sarah's story.

"No, I need a bone marrow donor," Sarah snapped, her own patience wearing thin. "I need someone to save my life, that's all!"

Ellen's eyes widened. "What?"

"A blood relative is most likely to be a compatible donor; you can't use just anyone, or believe me, I'd already have a volunteer." Sarah thought of her mom, who would have gladly undergone the procedure, and had to blink; she wouldn't cry in front of this stranger. "All my family and friends in California have already been tested, and no one matches. You'd be more likely to be a match, though it's still not automatic. But there's a much better chance. When the doctor talked about transplants, we didn't know where to find you; we didn't know who my birth parents were. We called Human Services in Nashville, and they said they'd do what they could."

Ellen looked away. "They sent me a letter," she murmured. "I didn't open it; I tore it up and threw it away. I was afraid someone else would see it."

She'd thrown away the letter—not knowing how important the message might be! Sarah felt a surge of anger. She took a deep breath, trying to stay calm.

"And now that you know?"

The silence seemed very long. A pulse in Ellen's throat throbbed visibly. "All right; I'll do it."

Sarah felt a wave of relief sweep over her; she almost missed the rest of Ellen's statement.

"As soon as the campaign is over, I'll have more time, and I can go—"

"No, I need it done now," Sarah protested, her voice sharp. "I don't have the time to wait; don't you understand? The disease gets worse every day;

if I get too ill, I'll be too weak to have any chance at all of the transplant working."

Ellen frowned. "But the campaign—"

"Is more important than my life?"

Ellen flushed. "No, of course not. But my husband has wanted this all his life, and he's really got a chance, this time. He ran once before and lost by a few hundred votes. I don't want to destroy his dream."

"And my chance to live a healthy life?" Sarah asked, her voice very low. "What about that?"

Ellen sighed. "All right. But I'll have to go to Nashville; I want it done as privately as possible. I'll call a doctor I know to set it up."

Sarah felt the first faint stirring of real hope. She told Ellen the name of Dr. Chavas and her hospital, where the test results should be sent. Ellen wrote it down on a small address book from her purse.

"And your children, they can be tested at the same time," Sarah pointed out.

"My children—no!" Ellen said, her voice rising. "No, they don't have to go through this. I won't have them subjected to any pain or risk."

"It isn't that bad," Sarah tried to explain. "They put you to sleep so you won't feel the needle that draws out some cells of bone marrow to test. There's a little risk, I guess, from the anesthesia— any surgery has some danger involved—but very little for a healthy person. And one of them might be the donor—you may not match."

"I thought you said—"

"I said the odds are much better, but it's not guaranteed," Sarah repeated. "Why can't the kids be tested? At least you could ask them?"

"No," Ellen said. "I can't. I'd have to tell them —everything."

Sarah stared at her as she slowly understood. "You mean you never told them anything about me? About your giving up a baby?"

Ellen turned her face away and stared at a tall maple rising above a nearby gravesite. "No, and I don't want them to know."

Sarah took a deep breath; she was shaken more deeply than she wanted to admit. Why hadn't she realized that Ellen would likely have kept her teen pregnancy a secret? Sarah knew two girls in her high school who had had babies, but things had been different years ago, she should have thought of that.

Just because her parents had always been open about Sarah's adoptive status, why had she assumed that Ellen would have been candid about her own situation? Sarah had been naive, she realized, and now she felt very foolish. Worse than foolish, she was Ellen's dirty little secret. "And your husband?"

Ellen lifted her chin and didn't answer.

No wonder Ellen wanted to keep everything quiet. Sarah looked at the woman's hands clasped so tightly on her purse; the knuckles were white, and her mouth was pressed into a thin hard line.

"Don't you trust him?" Sarah asked very quietly. "Just because you made one mistake—you were a kid, for crying out loud. Don't you think he loves you enough to accept what happened eighteen years ago?"

"Of course I do," Ellen snapped, still not meeting her eyes. "But he—he might not understand, he thought I was—not that kind of girl. You don't understand anything; you don't know what small towns are like, if you've grown up in a city. You don't know how people talk, and what they expect of you. . . . After all this time—how can I just walk up and say, 'By the way, Jim, I got pregnant when I was sixteen and gave the baby away—would you like to meet her?' And what would the papers make of this, just before the election? He'd lose any chance he had at winning. The embarrassment—my kids would be shocked and upset. I will not destroy my family!"

Sarah bit her lip, feeling her newborn hope slip away. It might not be enough, just having Ellen tested; it was only one hope, where there had been the possibility of more.

"What about my father?" she asked. "If you'd tell me who he is, I could try to find him, ask him to be tested. And he may have other children, too. Every blood relative tested gives me a better chance to find a donor."

Ellen's whole body stiffened. She took a deep breath, then shuddered. "No," she said. "Never."

"Wait!" Sarah protested, alarmed to see the

woman jump up and hurry toward the cemetery gate.

But Ellen didn't pause, didn't seem to hear. Sarah watched helplessly as the woman walked quickly, almost running, out of the graveyard and hurried to her parked car. She started the engine, grinding the starter, and pulled it away, driving too rapidly down the narrow street.

Had Sarah's last hope disappeared with her?

Chapter
Fifteen

Dear Diary,
   Ellen hasn't told her family that I exist. I shouldn't have been surprised, but still, it makes me feel as if I've been canceled out, negated. I'm only a bad memory to her; how can she hate me so much? She didn't ask me anything, if I'd been happy with my adopted family, if I have friends, if I do well in school, what I want to do with the rest of my life—if I should have a life, which doesn't look very likely.
   If she refuses to tell her children, if they're not tested, I've lost that many more chances to live.

   Sarah put down her pen and shut her diary. After the meeting with Ellen had ended so abruptly, she'd come back to her room at the bed and breakfast. Sarah felt very tired, and almost more discouraged than ever.
   But she had accomplished something. Ellen did say she'd be tested, Sarah reminded herself for the

tenth time. Maybe Ellen wouldn't change her mind about that part, at least; maybe she'd even be a compatible donor.

And then what? Would they have to wait till the political campaign was over for Ellen to take the time away for the procedure? She'd have to fly out to California where the transplant would be done, for best results. So far, Ellen didn't seem likely to cross the street for Sarah's sake. Oh, maybe she'd have the tests done, when it was convenient, when it wouldn't interfere with a campaign rally or luncheon or speech.

Sarah tried to hold back her rising anger at her birth mother. Wasn't Sarah as valuable as those other children she'd seen in front of the television cameras, posing with smiles and waves?

Her own mom thought so! Sarah felt so lonely and so alone. She thought of calling California, but if she called now, she'd break into tears and really upset her mom. Sighing, Sarah sat up. She wanted to go outside, to feel the fresh air on her face and sit in the warm sunshine. She felt cold, and she'd be inside for good all too soon if the transplant didn't occur, confined to a bed either in the hospital or at home.

It was so hard to avoid feeling sorry for herself, but Sarah knew that was a mistake; her depression would feed on itself, and she'd sink deeper into a morass of self-pity.

She'd seen some lawn furniture under the trees behind the big Victorian building. Sarah put her diary into her bag and walked outside. She found a comfortable chaise lounge with a padded blue and white cushion and sat down, putting her feet up.

Her face was in the shade, but the rest of her body was exposed to the welcome warmth of the afternoon sunshine. She heard a car pass on the street in front of the building, but back here it was peaceful and quiet. She tried not to think about all her problems. Instead, she thought of Mark and wondered what he would be doing right now, maybe having Sunday dinner with his mom and stepdad. She thought of her mom sitting patiently beside Nana's bed at the hospital. Thank goodness her grandmother's condition was improving.

Her thoughts drifted, and Sarah dozed. Then a sound behind her brought her abruptly awake. Someone had opened the backyard gate; she heard the sound of a squeaky hinge. A shadow loomed over her, and she gasped.

"Why did you come to see my mother?" a male voice spoke harshly.

Sarah sat up and looked back over her shoulder. He walked closer, circling the chaise lounge and standing over her. It was Ellen's oldest son—and he looked even more alarming now than he had when he'd driven the big tractor all too close to her scooter. Sarah felt a flicker of apprehension.

His blue eyes were squinted, and he frowned down at her. "Why are you bothering my mom?" he repeated, his voice louder. "I saw you speaking to her at the rally yesterday, and she came inside white as a ghost. Now she's all upset. What do you want? What did you say to her at the cemetery, to make her run out like that?"

"You were there?" Sarah asked.

He nodded. "I followed her after she left the luncheon today—I was in town, anyhow. And I wanted to know what was happening."

"You can't be old enough to have a driver's license," Sarah pointed out, looking at his smooth, freckled face. Some of her nervousness faded as she remembered how young he was.

He flushed. "I've been driving on the farm for years. Anyhow, nobody's going to take much notice around here," he said defiantly. "You didn't answer my question!"

"Why should I?" Sarah tried to think; according to Ellen, her son didn't know anything. What should she say?

"Mom's been nervous all day, and she looked tired this morning, as if she didn't sleep last night. She jumps every time the phone rings, and she looks afraid. And it's all since she talked to you."

Sarah didn't meet his angry gaze. "She talked to a lot of people at the rally," she said, still feeling her way. "How do you know it was me that upset her?"

He shook his head, brushing the suggestion aside. "I know everyone else who was there, except the reporters, and I heard all the interviews. No, I'm sure it was you. When Mom came inside after the rally, she watched you through the curtains until you walked away."

Sarah frowned, looking at his flushed, worried face. "Why didn't you ask her?"

He bit his lip, and this time he was the one who looked away. "I tried to, once, but Dad came in, and she changed the subject real fast. I didn't know what it was all about. I was afraid to ask again. I—I didn't want to make it worse."

He looked at her as if she were the enemy, and Sarah felt anger rising, numbing the pain she felt at being shut out, feared.

"Are you blackmailing my mother?" His voice wobbled with tension, but his eyes were accusing.

"You've been watching too much TV," she answered angrily. "Of course not!"

"But—"

"What a weird family you have," she snapped, "nothing but secrets between you. You're afraid to ask your own mom—why should I tell you anything? I'm glad I'm not part of your family!"

At once, she wished the words back, but the boy glared at her, suspicion in his blue eyes.

"What do you mean—'part of our family'? Why would you be?" He stared at her intently, and his mouth opened, then he swallowed hard.

"You look a little like—no, I don't believe it."

The confusion in his face was almost painful; Sarah looked away. What would Ellen say now, when she learned that Sarah had come too close to blurting out the whole thing? Would she be so angry that her secret had been exposed that she would refuse to be tested? This wasn't going to help Sarah, at all. And she was tired of the boy's antagonism.

"Go home and ask your mom," Sarah told him, lying back against the cushion. "I'm not telling you anything."

"Yes, you will!" All his frustration and anxiety seemed to turn to anger. He leaned over Sarah where she lay in the chaise lounge, unable to easily evade him. She gasped, but he grabbed her by the shoulders, shaking her hard.

"S-stop it!" Sarah's teeth chattered with the abrupt motion, and suddenly, to her dismay, she felt a spurt of blood from her nose.

She put up her hand, but the nosebleed was not easily stanched. The red was already staining her white T-shirt, and the boy stepped back, his face pale.

"I didn't—" he began, then backed away, his expression horrified.

Sarah knew what a ghastly sight she must look, and she felt both embarrassment and alarm. If she couldn't get the nosebleed to stop—

"What's this? Jamie Wright, what are you doing? Did you hit her? Well, I never!" The outraged voice of her landlady jarred them both.

Jamie shook his head, backing even farther away, then he panicked and ran for the gate.

"Lord, child, what a mess. What happened?" Mrs. Williams hurried up.

"It's just a nosebleed," Sarah mumbled. "I've had them before." The blood was running back into her throat, too, and she had to swallow hard, fighting back nausea at the sweet-sour taste of it. "Could you get me some ice, please?"

"Sure thing. You lie back."

Sarah dropped the chaise lounge flat and tilted her head back, pinching the top of her nose as the nurses had taught her.

In a short space the landlady was back, carrying a packet of sterile cotton to pack inside Sarah's nostril and an ice pack to place over the bridge of her nose. Mrs. Williams worked calmly, though her expression was worried. "Shouldn't we call a doctor, Sarah?"

"No," Sarah murmured. "It'll stop soon." She prayed it was true, that she didn't have to be taken into a doctor's office or, worse, an emergency room. So much for her low profile in this small town.

She lay very still for another twenty minutes, and finally the nosebleed seemed to have subsided.

Mrs. Williams, who had waited with her, sitting on a chair drawn up close to the chaise lounge, sighed in relief. "At least it was outside and not on the carpet," she said, practically. "Are you feeling better?"

Sarah didn't dare nod. "Yes, thank you. I'll just lie here awhile, to be safe."

"You call me if you need me," the landlady said. "I need to check on my muffins; they've been in the oven too long."

She went back inside, and Sarah relaxed a little, holding the ice bag to cover her nose. She shivered from the cold touch of it, but anything to stop the nosebleed. She shut her eyes and listened to a bird call from the trees; the air was warm and velvety. She had just begun to relax when she heard the gate creak again.

Should she call for the landlady?

But this time the steps were slow and hesitant. Sarah wasn't surprised to see Jamie Wright come back into her field of vision. His face was flushed with embarrassment, and he glanced at the ice bag that still covered much of her face, the bloodstains on her clothes.

"I didn't mean to hurt you," he said, gulping. "I'm sorry. You okay?"

"You didn't have to push me around," she murmured. Then, watching his eyes tense with worry, she relented. "I think it's stopped. Forget it."

She expected him to walk away again, his conscience eased. Instead he sat down on the chair that Mrs. Williams had pulled close, and he seemed to watch her.

"Are you related to my mom?"

Sarah stiffened in shock. She shut her eyes for a moment, trying to decide what to do.

"I'd think you were a cousin, except I know

there aren't any on her side of the family, not that I've heard of, anyhow. But when you frowned at me before, you looked so much like my mom when she's mad that you could almost—almost be my mother's daughter . . ." His voice was tight with suppressed emotion; it was almost a question.

Sarah could hardly breathe. His intuition had led him to the right answer, despite all the odds against it.

Yet after all the rejection Sarah had experienced today, his comment sparked an irrational anger inside her, as if Ellen could claim her so easily. "No," she snapped. "I'm not. I'm Margaret Davenport's daughter. Now go home; I'm not answering your questions. And if you touch me again, I'll call the landlady and have you arrested. That wouldn't help your dad's political ambitions very much, would it?"

Jamie winced. "I wouldn't—"

Sarah glared at him, and he faltered, then looked away. He stood up and retreated to the gate. In a moment she heard the sound of a pickup truck pulling away from the curb.

Sarah relaxed again. Despite her frustration, she wouldn't expose her birth mother's secret, not like this. Underneath Jamie's rudeness, she could glimpse a lingering hurt, perhaps as deep as her own.

Too many secrets.

Had it been a mistake to come here? Was even

saving her own life worth turning Ellen's family upside down, causing them so much pain?

Maybe Sarah had made the wrong choice, after all.

Chapter
Sixteen

Dear Diary,

Was it terribly selfish of me to come into Ellen's life, to risk upsetting her family? If my life wasn't at stake, I would never have tried to find her. I wonder if she believes that? And even if my life depends on it, how much pain can I cause everyone else?

I just don't know what to do anymore.

Sarah put away her diary, feeling confused and restless. She had been still as long as she could; the nosebleed seemed to have subsided. She emptied the ice bag of the melting ice and water and left it in her bathroom to dry. She washed her face very carefully, put her stained T-shirt in some cold water in the basin to soak, and found a clean shirt.

The pleasant bedroom felt confining; she was haunted by the image of herself confined to a bed, wasting away, cut off from the sunshine and fresh air. She wanted to be outside as long as she could.

Maybe tomorrow she would think about taking the bus back to Nashville and flying home to California. Maybe she'd accomplished as much here as she was going to do. She had found her birth mother, found at least one possible donor.

As for the rest, if she couldn't convince Ellen to tell her children—could Sarah take action on her own? She wasn't sure. She thought of the little girl she had seen at the rally, her expression so innocent. How would Sarah have felt at the age of six if she'd been told that her mother had another child Sarah had never heard of? Was it fair to Ellen's family to even consider such an option?

Sarah picked up her borrowed helmet and her purse and walked out of the bedroom. In the front hall she saw her landlady standing before the long mirror, adjusting a wide-brimmed hat. Instead of the jeans and shirt she'd been wearing earlier, she now had on a beige suit and heels.

"Are you going to the town meeting?" she asked Sarah. "Maybe it's not interesting to a teenager like you, but all the Nashville television crews will be there. We might end up on the ten o'clock news." She looked as excited as a kid, and despite her own worries, Sarah smiled at her enthusiasm.

"Where is it being held?"

"Down at the Elk Hall, just behind the sheriff's office, but the public's invited. Come on down, if you like, they're giving away free hot dogs and soda and cookies." She seemed to think that was sufficient inducement, and Sarah nodded, more amused than annoyed that Mrs. Williams would treat her like a hungry eight-year-old.

"Thank you for all your help this afternoon," she told her landlady. "I really appreciated it."

Mrs. Williams smiled. "I'm just glad you're feeling better, though you still look a mite peaked. Lord, you gave me a real scare, you know, with blood all over the place. But nosebleeds can be like that; my oldest boy had trouble with them when he was small. I've mopped up plenty."

Sarah nodded. "Thanks again. And I hope you end up on the news," she called as the woman headed toward the front door.

Should she go down to the meeting and hope for another chance to talk to Ellen? Would all the children be there? She didn't particularly want to meet Jamie Wright again, face-to-face, but her half brother could hardly assault her in a public place, could he? And anyhow, he'd seemed genuinely contrite when he'd returned to apologize.

Sarah made a decision. She glanced into the mirror herself, saw that she was even paler than usual, and reached into her purse for some makeup. She applied some pink lipstick and a little blush, trying to hide her pallor. Then she pulled on the borrowed helmet and walked out back to the motor scooter. She started the engine and drove back through town, not rushing, enjoying the wind on her face and the golden afternoon sunlight washing over her, as if it could replace the life and energy she was losing so rapidly.

It was easy enough to find the Elk Hall; there were cars and pickup trucks parked all along the adjoining streets, and again Sarah saw the TV vans with their bright logos.

She parked her little scooter and walked slowly toward the building; music was playing and someone had hung bunting and balloons around the front door. The election signs were large: ELECT JAMES WRIGHT FOR STATE REPRESENTATIVE; HE'S THE RIGHT MAN FOR THE JOB. Rival signs vied for space: ELECT TOMMY J. SMITHFIELD: THE MAN WITH THE KNOW-HOW.

Sarah nodded at the smiling campaign workers at the entrance who were handing out leaflets.

A woman in a straw campaign hat glanced at her, as if not certain if Sarah was eighteen and eligible to vote, then apparently decided not to take a chance. "Welcome, dear," she said, her smile practiced.

Accepting the campaign flyer, Sarah smiled in return. The crowd milled around the rows of folding chairs, and there were tables of food along the back. At least a hundred people, maybe more, filled the long hall to capacity.

She wandered around the edge of the crowd, looking for a familiar face. A podium had been set up in front, and several men in business suits stood on the stage, talking to each other. The candidates themselves seemed to be working the crowd; she recognized Jim Wright from the rally at the farm. He was shaking hands and greeting as many of the audience as possible before the speeches began. He was coming her way; Sarah felt suddenly exposed, as if her face would give away all the secrets Ellen was trying so desperately to keep hidden. Sarah turned away and pretended to read the leaflet in her hand, then headed for the food tables.

She accepted a hot dog and a paper cup of cola, then found an empty seat at the back of the rows. More people were seating themselves now, and there was a man at the front calling for quiet in the hall.

Where was Ellen? Sarah glanced around, but didn't see her birth mother. She chewed on the lukewarm hot dog, ate as much of it as she could manage, then took a gulp of soda.

The music blared more loudly, then faded. The TV crews with their cameras and microphones on long booms moved closer to the stage, ready to film. The assembled crowd finally paid attention to the man at the mike and the talk died, then Sarah could hear the man at the loudspeaker plainly. He had been introducing a group of city and county officials gathered at the back of the platform.

Then he went on, "Thanks for coming out tonight, folks. We're happy to see so many people eager to take advantage of their American heritage and be informed voters, ready to make a choice when election day rolls around. Now, you didn't come here to listen to me ramble on, so let me introduce the first candidate."

Sarah's thoughts wandered as the first man

made his speech. She glanced around the platform, trying to find Ellen and her children. There they were, at the back, behind a group of local officials. Did Jamie look distracted? Ellen was not smiling; she didn't look as calm and in control as the first time Sarah had seen her. Was their encounter at the cemetery still playing over and over within her mind, just as it did in Sarah's?

The hall was too hot, packed with so many people. It was hard to listen to the speeches. In the row in front of Sarah, a baby cried, the mother tried to shush her, then stood up to slip outside.

Sarah watched them go, feeling a pang. The mother looked annoyed, but she still held the infant carefully, lovingly. Mother and child—Sarah had a mother, but she was far away, and she wanted her presence very badly.

She would go back home tomorrow; she'd been here long enough. What else could she accomplish, anyhow?

The last speech finally ended, and the families were being introduced. Ellen stepped up to the mike. Sarah drew her attention back to the stage.

"Thank you for listening to my husband's speech tonight; it's my pleasure to be a part of his campaign, to help a man that I respect so much. I know he means what he says, I know he wants to help the ordinary people of this state and this district. We support the family, as my husband has told you; nothing can be more important than strong family values. . . ."

The irony of it was inescapable. Sarah watched her birth mother intently, forgetting all the people who sat between them. And as if her fixed stare had drawn Ellen's gaze, Ellen glanced across the seated audience and suddenly paused, as if noticing Sarah for the first time.

Did she really see Sarah at the back, through all the other people? Ellen's voice faltered, and her cheeks suddenly flushed. There was an uncomfortable silence; Sarah could hear the click of the cameras rolling in front of the stage, their mechanical eyes recording all the strain on Ellen's face. Some of the people in the crowd shifted, as if embarrassed by this moment of apparent stage fright.

Sarah knew better. It wasn't just an attack of nervousness in front of a crowd—Ellen was looking at Sarah.

"Thank you for coming," Ellen finished, her voice weak, her cheeks still red. She walked back to join her family, and she seemed to tremble.

The other candidate's wife said a few words, and the moderator thanked everyone for coming. People in the crowd stood, stretched, chatted to each other, and some drifted foward to shake their chosen candidate's hand one more time.

Ellen stood at the back, with one hand on her daughter's shoulder, as if ready to protect her brood. Frowning fiercely, Jamie Wright stood close to his mother and brother and sister. His face looked pale, the freckles standing out in vivid relief.

Ellen thought Sarah was a danger, a threat. Sarah shut her eyes, sighing. Should she try to speak to Ellen again? How could she? In their eyes, she was the enemy; Ellen and her family had closed ranks against her. Sarah felt very alone. She sat still, not moving, and as people around her stood up, she soon lost sight of Ellen and her children as the milling spectators blocked her view.

Sarah felt ashamed. She hadn't come here to hound anyone, to make Ellen miserable and afraid. If her birth mother was so worried about making Sarah's existence known—what choice did Sarah have?

When did saving yourself cease to be an excuse for destroying someone else's happiness?

She knew now what she had to do. If Ellen refused to tell her family—well, Sarah couldn't do it, not by herself. She couldn't rush in and tell little kids—the two youngest, at least, were little—a secret they didn't know about their own mother. And what if Ellen's husband really was shocked, really didn't forgive her? Did some men still act like that? Would the long-suppressed secret destroy Ellen's marriage? Sarah didn't want that on her conscience.

She wanted to get away from all these people. Sarah stood up, thankful to be unnoticed in the noisy crowd, and slipped out of the hall. She walked back to her parked scooter and pulled the helmet back on. She wanted quiet; she wanted to be alone.

The cemetery was only a little farther down the street. She drove the extra blocks, then slowed the scooter and pulled onto the grass beside the road. She turned off the engine and slipped her helmet off, leaving it on the scooter's seat. She walked slowly through the gateway. A tall security light shone in the middle of the grassy space, leaving shadows around the edges.

Perhaps she should have been nervous about a graveyard at night, with the quiet headstones rising out of the dimness. But when you were facing death itself, in all its cold reality, childish Halloween fantasies didn't seem alarming anymore.

Sarah sat down on the first bench, just beyond the gateway, and listened to a distant hum of crickets and a frog hur-uping somewhere in the darkness. Were you really at peace after you died? If the quiet bodies in the coffins were just husks, empty vessels, where did the souls—the spirits— go? Surely a human soul was too strong, too big, to die with the fragile flesh.

Her mom had told her that she believed in heaven; Sarah wished she could be certain. Her father would be there, waiting for her. Yet, she wasn't ready to die. She had wanted so much more from her life . . .

She was so deep in her thoughts that she didn't hear the other person approaching until she sensed someone very close. Sarah jumped, startled by the woman coming out of the shadows.

It was Ellen Wright who stood in the entrance to

the footpath. Her face was shaded, and Sarah couldn't see her expression.

Sarah raised her chin; why had she come back?

"I saw you leave on the scooter," Ellen said quietly. "I followed you here. I thought—"

She faltered, and Sarah waited. Her faint rush of hope faded almost as soon as it had appeared. Ellen still sounded defensive, hostile.

"You don't have to worry," Sarah told her, hearing the heaviness in her own voice. "I'm not going to bother you or your children anymore. I'm going home tomorrow."

Ellen took a deep breath. "I thought I should explain—" But again she paused; whatever she had to say seemed too much for her self-control; she was breathing too fast, and her whole body was rigid.

"You don't have to explain anything; I know you hate me." Sarah wrapped her arms around her own body, trying not to tremble.

"You don't know what it was like," Ellen said, bitterness thick in her words. "My parents—my father always preaching to me, how I had to set an example. My mother giving me anxious looks, making me feel guilty if I did the least thing—because people would talk, and that would reflect on my father, and the church itself. I never had a chance to find out who I was, not ever; I had to be the preacher's daughter, always perfect. I got so tired of doing what everyone else said . . ."

She folded her arms across her chest. "One

night, two of my friends were going to a beer joint on the edge of town; there was a dance with a real band. They asked me to go, too. I climbed out of my bedroom window after my parents thought I was asleep and drove off in my friend's old jalopy. It was an adventure; I felt as if I was doing something wonderfully wicked.

"The beer joint was small and dark and dirty, but there was this man there—he had on a black leather jacket, and he had a real tattoo on his arm, and a dark mustache and long hair. He asked me to dance—it was like a movie, Marlon Brando, you know. I felt like another person altogether, free and grown-up, doing something exciting, something forbidden."

Ellen was trembling now, and Sarah could hear a catch in her voice, but she didn't dare interrupt.

"He told me I was pretty; he offered to give me a ride on his motorcycle—I'd never been on one; my parents wouldn't allow it. So I said yes; I thought we'd have a short ride, maybe he would kiss me . . . But he took me ten miles out of town, to a dark, deserted back road, and he wanted to have sex. I said no, I was scared now, I begged him to take me back . . . but he pushed me down onto the grass beside the road, and he raped me. Then he rode away and left me there, hurting and scared and so ashamed. . . ."

Sarah felt Ellen's pain so deeply it made her cold inside, and the shock of the revelation left her numb. She was the product of a rape? No wonder Ellen didn't want to see her, know her.

"When I got home, my father called our family doctor," Ellen said, very low. "He promised not to tell anyone. But he didn't do what a hospital would have done, and later, when I found I was pregnant, I didn't know what to do. My parents wouldn't even consider an abortion; they decided that I would go to stay with my aunt in Memphis, in a big city where no one would know me. They told everyone I had scarlet fever; I had the baby there and gave it up to be adopted. When it was born, I never saw it, never held it. It was all a nightmare, and I just wanted it over."

She was only an "it" to her birth mother, Sarah thought dimly, still paralyzed with shock.

"So about the man who begot you, I don't even know his last name." Ellen's voice was harsh and ragged. "I can't tell you anything to help you find him, and I really don't think you want to."

"Didn't you go to the police?" Sarah asked, her voice trembling. Her fists were clinched, trying to control her own anguish, as well as the pain that overflowed from Ellen's tense body.

"Police would have meant publicity, and everyone would have known. Besides, my father said they would say it was my fault, for going off with a man I didn't know. The whole town would have been talking, and people would have blamed me. They weren't talking about date rape on every talk show eighteen years ago, you know." Ellen stared away into the darkness, not meeting Sarah's eyes.

"I believed my father; I thought it was my fault, and my sin. After the baby was born, I came back and finished high school, but I was afraid to go off to college, as I'd planned. I was afraid of everything; I'd sit in my room and cry, all alone. When Jim asked me out, when he wanted to marry me—he was kind, and he was older, and he made me feel safe." She drew a ragged breath. "I don't hate you; at least, I've tried hard not to. But I didn't want to tell anyone about that night, certainly not my husband or my children. I wanted to forget it ever happened."

"And have you?" Sarah asked quietly, the words forced out of her. "Before I came, have you managed to forget?"

The question hung on the night air, and she saw the deep shudder that passed over Ellen's whole body.

"No," she whispered. "I think of it every day, and I hurt all over again. I relive it all in my nightmares and I feel the fear and the guilt."

The idea of being the product of such pain made Sarah sick to her stomach. She stood up and walked away, not wanting to watch Ellen's tortured face.

"Don't worry about me," Sarah told her. "I'm going home. Maybe dying is the best thing I can do for you."

Chapter
Seventeen

Dear Diary,
  Even though I knew nothing about my birth parents, I always imagined they must have had at least a moment of love between them. I thought I might have been born to a teenager too young to raise me, or to a woman with too many children already and no money to feed another . . .
  But I never imagined a rape—just the thought of it makes me sick to my stomach.
  I was born from an assault, from pain and indignity and fear. Instead of growing from a loving union, I was conceived in hatred, in a vicious attack on a helpless girl.
  No wonder I have cancer. I started with a moment of evil, how could I hope to grow into something healthy and strong? Maybe I deserve to die.

  Her hand was shaking; she put down the pen and the diary. Sarah felt very cold; a chill shook her body and her teeth chattered. She lay down across the bed and pulled up the thick quilt that lay folded at the bottom of her bed. For several minutes she shook, racked with chills, then the spasm passed, and she felt the flush of fever.

Pushing back the covers, Sarah thought of her antibiotic tablets, of the Tylenol to reduce the fever. She should get up and go to the bathroom for some water, find the pills in her purse. But it seemed like too much effort. Maybe, as she had written in her diary, she didn't deserve to live.

To have come from so much evil—she felt tainted, dirty. How could she look at herself in the mirror ever again? She wasn't even sure who she was anymore.

Child of rape.

Another chill rushed through her, and now she was cold again, shivering. She pulled the quilt back up and huddled beneath the heavy cotton coverlet, pulling her legs up into a ball, still shaking.

She shut her eyes and saw Ellen, young and afraid, trying to push away a dark-haired man in a leather jacket. His face was lost in the darkness, but Ellen was crying out . . .

Sarah shuddered and tried not to see the rest of the assault. Evil, she was the product of an evil act.

She could look inside herself and almost see a hidden core of darkness that she'd never suspected before. No wonder the cancer was coursing through her bloodstream, sapping her of energy and the chance to live. She had been tainted from the beginning—from the first moment of sperm meeting egg. Perhaps the same kind of sick rage lurked inside her own body, her soul, just waiting to emerge.

Was she a monster, too, like the pitiful excuse of a man who had been willing to assault a frightened girl? She couldn't call him "father"; it made a mockery of the word.

Sarah sobbed, the tears sliding down her cheeks and dampening the pillow beneath her. She was still drawn up into a tight knot beneath the heavy covering, but the cold wouldn't leave her. What would her mom say to this awful news—would she love Sarah as much when she knew the shameful secret behind her birth?

What about Mark—how could she ever tell Mark the truth? He would look at her differently, with amazement and distaste. Sarah sobbed again and put one hand to her mouth, trying to hold back the inarticulate sounds of her grief. She felt truly bereft, and the harsh moans seemed to come from deep inside, from a bottomless grief she couldn't control. She didn't want anyone to hear, to come and ask her what was wrong—how could she explain this?

She wished she'd never come to this little town —never sought out her birth mother—never asked about her birth father. It would have been better to stay in California and die with her family and friends around her, Sarah thought. She'd never

have known the terrible truth about her begin-
nings, and at least she could have died in peace.

Now her own picture of herself had changed,
blurred, and she felt as if she had been dropped
into a maelstrom of darkness. It was like being
abandoned in a twisting tunnel, not knowing which
way to turn for light. She was lost in her own grief
and shock, and there seemed no way out, none at
all.

The pain inside her was greater than her physical discomfort, even though chills shook her whole
body. She shut her eyes and wished for an end,
wished for all of it to go away. She only wanted to
go home to her mother, and now perhaps even
that refuge would not be the same, once she'd
shared the awful news. Sarah had never felt so
alone.

The chill finally died, and the fever returned.
She was hot again, and she pushed the heavy quilt
back, still weak and sick but so anguished that she
pushed too hard, shaking the duffel bag that had
been sitting forgotten at the foot of the bed.

The bag shifted, and last year's high school annual slid out. Sarah eyed it dimly, fever making her
vision blur and waver. But the patch of red was a
sign of her old life, the old Sarah who had been
loved and happy and secure. Instinctively, she
reached out for it, touched the hard rectangular
shape, pulled it up to hold next to her.

For a minute she simply relished the familiar
feel of the textured cover. Then, hot and flushed,

she managed to open the cover and glance inside. Where was the Baby Photo page, where students could contribute a picture of themselves? She turned the pages till she found the snapshot she sought—Sarah as a grinning toddler, in a white hat and flowered sundress, her mom and dad beaming at her as they all sat on a blanket in the park.

They all looked so happy, the picture of a loving family. Sarah had always loved that photo—it was why she had selected it for the annual page. That smiling little girl didn't look evil, Sarah thought dimly. Was her inner core of corruption so well hidden?

She trembled, and the pages fell shut; she reached to open the book again and paused at the inside cover, which was covered with her friends' end-of-the-year messages.

Dear Sarah,

Thanks for helping me with extra flag practice; I would never have learned all the routines without you. It was a fun year. Your friend always,

Annette

Yo, Sarah,

Stay sweet and sassy till next year; we'll be the coolest senior class ever, and you'll be the best of the best. You're my kind of gal!

Serji

Hi, Sarah,

Thanks for being my best friend for ever and ever; for not telling my secrets, for listening to me when I was down, for standing up for me with you-know-who, for lending me your best dress for my first date with Don. We'll always be sisters of the heart. Love,

Maria

Dear Sarah,

You're very special; I'm looking forward to knowing you a lot better. I hope to write a whole page in your annual next year—

Mark

There were more, from good friends and casual acquaintances, but Sarah found that she had stopped crying. The grief was still there inside her, for the terrible tragedy of the rape, for the darkness of her conception. But her panic had faded. The girl who had friends like these, friends who cared about her and who saw good things inside her—surely this girl wasn't evil?

Maybe she was still Sarah, still the person she'd always thought herself. Sarah read more of the scribbled messages and jokes, then shut the yearbook and held it close to her chest. She felt so hot and her mouth was dry as cotton.

In a few minutes she put down the book and struggled to her feet. Swaying dizzily, she held on to the bedside table till her head cleared, then she made her way to the bathroom. She splashed cool water on her flushed face, glancing at her red nose and swollen eyelids only briefly, then filled a paper cup with water. She drank quickly, then refilled it and brought it back to the bed, so she could take her pills.

Then she lay back against the bed, sighing. Maybe, maybe she could still be herself, put aside the knowledge of Ellen's secret, go on with her life —if she had any life to speak of left to her.

But she had to tell her mom, see if Margaret Davenport was horrified, too, if she would feel any differently about her adopted daughter.

What time was it? Sarah pushed the small clock on the bedside table around till she could peer at its digital face. Past ten o'clock. She could just make out the faint hum of the television from the front sitting room. Had Mrs. Williams made it onto the television screen via the clips from the town hall meeting? It seemed aeons ago that the landlady had primped in front of the mirror in preparation for the big night.

Sarah waited almost an hour, then when the noise had faded and she felt that everyone else had gone to bed, she stood up, still weak and shaky, and headed for the sitting room and the phone.

The fever had abated, though she was still warm. But at least the floor didn't tilt beneath her feet this time. She dialed the number quickly, wanting this over with, wanting to know the worse.

"Mom?"

"Sarah, are you all right?"

"How's Nana?" Sarah said, trying to put off the awful news a moment longer.

"She's improving; she walked down the hall today," her mother said. "How are you; you don't sound well. Are you worse? I wish you'd come home, Sweetheart."

"I'm going to, soon," Sarah agreed. "Mom, I talked to Ellen again; she told me something else."

The silence stretched; there seemed to be an obstruction in her throat; Sarah swallowed hard, trying to force the words.

"Sarah, what is it?"

"She was raped. Ellen, I mean," Sarah said, her voice hardly more than a croak. "I was born of a rape, Mom."

"Oh, Sarah."

What did she hear in her mom's voice? Sadness, shock, revulsion, withdrawal? Sarah rushed on.

"It makes me feel so terrible, knowing . . . I was afraid, almost to tell you. I was afraid you couldn't love me as much, if you knew—" Her throat closed up again, and Sarah couldn't go on.

"Sarah," her mother said, this time more firmly. "I'm terribly sorry for Ellen, that she was subjected to such a crime, but it doesn't affect you."

"It has to," Sarah muttered, still not able to talk clearly.

"You are still the same precious, beautiful, wonderful baby that we adopted, your father and I. You're still just as blessed, just as much of a miracle to us. You've grown up to be compassionate and loyal and intelligent and brave, coping courageously with an illness that not even adults can always handle. You've been the best part of my life for the last seventeen and a half years, Sarah Elizabeth Davenport, and there is no way that I could love you any less, not ever!" Her mother finished fiercely.

This time, Sarah was too choked up to answer, but the tears in her eyes were from relief and happiness. "I love you, too," she was finally able to whisper. "But, Mom, do you think that was what caused the cancer—this awful wounding—did it twist my whole DNA into the wrong patterns?"

"No one knows what causes cancer to start, Sweetheart; it's probably a lot of different things. In fifty years or a hundred, perhaps the doctors will be able to answer that question. But I don't believe it's a curse put on you by your conception. You have the right to exist, you have the right to shape your own life, to have it healthy and good."

The strength of her mother's tone comforted her, soothed some of her wildest fears. Sarah took a deep breath.

"Please come home, Sarah."

"I will. I'll check on the plane schedules and the bus times in the morning," Sarah promised.

They talked a few more minutes, then Sarah hung up the phone, feeling as if a great burden had been lifted from her shoulders. But there was one more person she needed to talk to.

She dialed again, holding the phone receiver tightly. "Mark, it's Sarah."

"Sarah, what's wrong?"

"Mark, my—the woman who gave birth to me— she told me about my father; she doesn't even know his whole name—she was raped, Mark."

"Oh, man," he said, very low. "That's heavy, Sarah. You okay?"

"No, I feel terrible." Sarah swallowed a sob. "I told Mom, and she told me it doesn't make any difference, she wouldn't love me any less, but I was afraid—"

"You think I would feel different about you, because of that?" His voice rose, and Sarah blushed, thankful he couldn't see her face. "Sarah, you know better. It doesn't change anything. I don't care what happened to that woman—I mean, I'm sorry about the rape and all, but—what I care about is you, Sarah, you, right now."

She smiled at last, and this time she could speak more easily, knowing the force of his words came from genuine concern. "I'm glad."

"You keep your head on straight. You've got enough to worry about without all that junk from years ago. And, Sarah, hurry home."

When she replaced the phone, Sarah walked slowly back to bed, but despite the dimness of the bedroom, she no longer felt engulfed by darkness.

Whatever had happened years ago, she was Sarah, still loved, still valued.

She turned off the lamp, but she tucked her yearbook under her pillow before she shut her eyes.

Chapter
Eighteen

Dear Ellen,

Thank you for seeing me last night and telling me the truth, finally. It hurt to hear it, but it helps me to understand a lot.

Thank you for agreeing to be tested as a possible bone marrow donor. Please do it soon, if you can; my time is running out. You gave me the gift of life once; perhaps you can do it again.

If you decide to tell your children, and if they agree to be tested, I would be very grateful. But if you decide not to tell them, I won't interfere. I'm not trying to hurt them; even with my own life at stake, I can't do that to little kids.

I'm going back to California tomorrow. You have my doctor's name and the hospital; please send the test results there, and they'll contact you. I won't write to you again; you have the right to your life and your privacy.

I'm going back to my life, and I hope I get to

keep it. Thank you for giving me up to a good family; I've been very happy, and I've been loved.

Sarah thought a moment, then signed her name. She addressed the envelope and added a stamp—she had bought a couple from her landlady—and took the letter and her postcard to Maria out to the big mailbox on the corner.

She had already called the Nashville airport. To her disappointment, today's only direct afternoon flight to Los Angeles was full. The bus wouldn't get her back to Nashville in time to catch the morning flights, and she didn't feel well enough to cope with a change of planes in Denver or Dallas or Santa Fe.

"What about tomorrow?" she'd asked.

"We have seats open on that flight," the woman at the other end of the line said cheerfully.

So Sarah had made a reservation for tomorrow afternoon. Now she thought about what she had to do before she left Pleasant Hills. She had to return the scooter to the gargage and pay the man for the rental, but how would she get down to the gas station to catch the bus?

Mrs. Williams came through and glanced into the front room. "You're up bright and early this morning; ready for breakfast?"

Sarah nodded. "Yes, thank you, I'll be right there."

Despite the early hour in California, she called

her mom and told her which flight she'd be on. Margaret Davenport sounded relieved. "I'll be glad to have you safely home, Sweetheart."

"Me, too," Sarah agreed.

"And perhaps Ellen will turn out to be a compatible donor; I'll be praying hard," her mom said.

Sarah shut her eyes for a moment—she was almost afraid to hope.

"Put your room bill at the bed and breakfast on the credit card; I don't want you to run out of money before you get back. And I'll be at the airport to pick you up," her mom told her.

"Is it safe to leave Nana? I could get a cab, if I need to, and Mark will come if he's out of school in time."

"No, I want to be there," her mother told her. "And your grandmother's doing much better."

It made Sarah warm inside, just thinking of getting off the plane and seeing her mother's welcoming smile, her arms outstretched.

"I'll see you tomorrow," she said before she hung up.

"I love you, Sarah," her mom said. "Be careful."

"I love you, too."

She replaced the receiver, relieved at the thought of going home. She'd slept restlessly and woken early; her fever had receded, but she was still overly warm. Sarah was afraid her physical condition was getting worse; if she had any hope of the transplant working, it would have to be done soon. Maybe Ellen would heed her warnings and get the tests done quickly. Maybe she would be compatible. Too many maybes, but it was all Sarah could hope for.

Sighing, she went into the sunny dining room and managed to eat a light, fluffy biscuit spread with butter and strawberry jam. She drank some milk and ate a slice of melon, then pushed her plate back.

"Is there a local taxi service?" she asked her landlady when Mrs. Williams came to take away the plates.

"Bless you, no; we're not big enough to have a taxicab. What do you need, dear?"

"I'm leaving tomorrow," Sarah told her. "I'll need to take the scooter back to the garage before I go, and I really don't feel like walking several miles to catch the bus to Nashville."

"No indeed," Mrs. Williams said, glancing at Sarah's flushed cheeks. "I'll take you up to catch the bus myself; it's no trouble."

"Oh, thank you," Sarah said. "You're very kind."

"I want you to get home in one piece," her landlady said firmly. "I can see you're not feeling very well; you need to get home and rest, get back in shape."

She needed more than rest, but Sarah didn't want to explain it all; she didn't enjoy the surprise and pity that came when people learned about her cancer.

She went back to her room and took a nap, then

spent the afternoon lying in the backyard on the chaise lounge, listening to the birds sing in the trees, watching the pattern of light and shadows beneath the shade trees. Much of her tension had gone. She had done as much as she could do, and she'd chosen not to go any further. That was her right, Sarah told herself, not to disrupt Ellen's family, upset her children. Sarah had made her choice, and knowing that she would be home soon relieved her loneliness.

At dinnertime, she got back on the scooter and rode down to the tearoom. This time, she felt no weight on her conscience. She sat down at one of the small tables and ordered a bowl of soup and some of the cheesecake in the glass case.

Mary Anne came out to take her order, and Sarah looked up at her over the small menu. "I'm going back to California tomorrow."

She thought the stout woman relaxed a little. "I see. I hope you've enjoyed your stay here," she said formally.

Sarah raised her brows. "It's been enlightening," she said, meeting Mary Anne's brown eyes. "But it's time for me to go home."

The woman nodded and didn't answer, but she brought her an extra large piece of the cheesecake.

Sarah hid a smile and ate as much as she could, savoring the tastes of the homemade soup and the rich fluffy dessert. When she started chemotherapy again, the unpleasant taste in her mouth would likely return, spoiling what little appetite she had.

When she finished her meal and paid the bill, she drove one last time down to the graveyard and walked over to the graves of her grandparents.

She stared at the double headstone with its formal engraving. Her grandfather had been so upright, and such a coward. If he and his wife had been more understanding with their daughter, a little more human, a little less concerned about how their small town would judge her behavior, perhaps the rape would never have occurred in the first place.

But how much blame could you lay on someone else? If Ellen hadn't sneaked out with her friends, if she hadn't gone off with the strange man—the rape would also never have happened, with all its tragic repercussions.

But if it hadn't happened, then Sarah wouldn't be here today. And she wanted to have been born, to be alive, even if she was fighting for her life, fighting to defeat the cancer. What she'd had of her life had been good; she just wanted more of it.

Good and evil, pain and happiness, tragedy and joy—it was all mixed up together, and she couldn't see where the line could be drawn. It was a paradox, a puzzle as old as time itself, perhaps, and too difficult for Sarah to decipher.

But she was here, and her mom loved her, even if Ellen would never be able to. And Mark cared for her, too, might love her totally one day. Would he be able to stand by her through the difficult times to come? Sarah sighed at the thought; a serious illness took its toll on everyone, the patient and her family and friends. Maria had never abandoned her, surely Mark would prove as loyal. She hoped so.

She felt very tired; it was time to go back and lie down again. The illness was pushing forward, marching through her veins like a conquering army. And there were so few defenses left to raise —unless Ellen proved to be a compatible donor.

Worrying didn't help, Sarah told herself. She walked slowly back to her scooter, pulled on her helmet, and drove back to the bed and breakfast. She looked at the big old houses along Main Street, the small businesses, the quiet streets— she'd always remember this small town where her birth mother had grown up.

But Sarah's home was in Los Angeles, in Marina Del Rey, with the busy crowded avenues and apartment buildings, the bristling forest of masts that rose from the sailboats lined up at the marina, the beaches covered with tourists and locals both, the hum of a big city all around them. That was home, and the thought brought a pang of homesickness with it. Soon, tomorrow, Sarah was going home.

She parked the scooter at the bed and breakfast and went to her bedroom and napped, reading a magazine she found in the front sitting room, and spending the rest of the evening quietly.

The next morning she woke early, ate, and repacked her one duffel bag, impatient to be off. But there were still several hours to wait till it was time to return the scooter and have Mrs. Williams drive her down to catch the bus. Too restless to stay inside, Sarah wandered out to the chaise lounge in the backyard.

She lay back and shut her eyes, trying to relax. The creak of the side gate made her glance over her shoulder. She was startled to see Jamie Wright walking toward her. Instinctively, she tensed. It was too much like the first meeting they'd had, which had ended with an explosion of temper.

But he wasn't frowning this time; if anything, he looked a little nervous. He stopped a few feet from her lounge chair and cleared his throat.

"I'm glad I got here before you left," he said.

Sarah looked at him in surprise. "How did you know I was leaving?"

"Mom got your letter this morning."

"She told you?" Sarah sat up straighter. "She told you about me?"

He nodded. "Not at first. But she read the letter and started to cry, then she got up and went into the bedroom, and my dad went to see what was wrong. They shut the door and talked a long time. I waited around, and Bryan and Lauren were real nervous, but I suspected—well—that it had something to do with you."

Sarah held her breath. Was he angry? He didn't sound accusing. "And?"

"In a while, they came out holding hands, and

she told us, about the rape, about having a baby, about giving you up when she was sixteen."

Sarah exhaled slowly, and some of the tension inside her eased. "Were you—was it a big shock?"

"Yes and no. I never expected to hear that I had a half sister I'd never heard about." His tone was wry instead of angry, and he sat down on the nearest lawn chair, not quite meeting her gaze. "But I always knew there was something wrong somewhere. Mom never talked much about her high school years, not like Dad, and when someone else mentioned those days, her face would close up. And sometimes, if you asked the wrong question—it was like walking across a field barefoot, not knowing when you're going to step on a sharp rock —she'd get angry over nothing at all. It's better to know, I think."

"I'm glad you don't hate me," Sarah murmured.

He shook his head. "She told us about you being sick and needing a bone marrow transplant."

Sarah flushed, but he went on quickly. "Mom's going in to be tested the day after tomorrow, and I'm going, too."

Sarah felt tears blur her vision. "You are?"

He nodded. "Bryan will, too, and maybe Lauren. She's afraid it will hurt, you know? But I think if we do it, she'll decide to as well. I don't want you to die, Sarah. I felt so bad that I made your nose bleed the other day. I just didn't know— I thought you were trying to hurt my mom. I didn't know she was your mother, too."

He looked at her, a little pale beneath his freckles, and Sarah tried hard to smile at him, but the tears of relief still threatened to overflow.

"You'll be okay, won't you, if you get the transplant, if one of us is compatible and can give you the bone marrow you need?" His voice was anxious.

Sarah swallowed again, trying to control her voice. "I hope so. It doesn't work for everyone, and the side effects can be very difficult; I'll be sick for weeks. Some people die after a transplant. But I intend to live, if I just get the chance."

"I want you to live," he told her. "I really wanted to see you again before you left, so I could tell you that. And I admit, I was curious about you, too. I mean, are your parents good to you? Do you like school? Do you have a lot of friends?"

Sarah grinned. All the questions she had thought her birth mother might ask, and instead it was Jamie who wanted to know.

"My mom is great, and my dad was, too. He died of a heart attack two years ago. I'm pretty good in school; I'm usually on the honor roll—"

"Me, too," he interrupted.

"And I was cocaptain of the tall flags last year; we have a lot of fun when we go off to football games, riding the bus and singing and telling jokes and just acting silly. I want to enjoy my senior year, if I get the chance. I want to go to college. Mostly, I just want to live. Maybe one of you will be able to give me that chance." Sarah took a deep breath.

Jamie looked at her, his expression suddenly diffident. "Do you have any brothers or sisters?"

"No," Sarah told him. "Just me."

He looked at a bee hovering over a flower in the border beyond their chairs. "You think maybe you'd want to write to me, sometimes?"

Sarah looked at him in surprise, but he didn't look up, just watched the bee as it skimmed over the flowers.

"I'd like that," she said.

Chapter
Nineteen

Dear Diary,

I can't believe I've been back in California for only two weeks; it seems like a year ago I made the trip to Tennessee, and yet it's changed my whole life.

Ellen and all her children were tested, but it was Jamie who turned out to be a compatible donor. He called me when they told him, just before the doctor called us, and he sounded really proud that he could be the one to help me. I owe him so much; he's giving me the chance to live. He'll fly out in three days for the procedure, and when he's out of the hospital, Mark and Maria and some of my friends are going to take him around to all the fun places, Disneyland and Universal Studios and the works—give him a real vacation before he goes back home.

Me, I've already had a ton of tests. They've put the PICC (central catheter) back into my chest for all the tubes and stuff. Tomorrow the countdown begins, six days till the actual transplant. I go into isolation, and no one but my mom and grandmother (and maybe Mark, I've been begging the doctors!) will get to come in, all scrubbed and dressed in sterile white suits and masks. I'll start all the chemotherapy and radiation that occurs before the transplant itself; my hair will fall out again. I know it's dumb to worry about the small stuff, but I hate for Mark to see me like that.

I should be worrying about afterward, 'cause I know I'll be really sick for a while. But I'll get past that, and I'm going to recover and get well. I've made up my mind. Jamie's giving me this chance, and I intend to make the most of it.

Sarah put down her pen and closed her diary. She looked around the hospital room; it was filled with balloons and flowers and funny cards. Most of her friends had come by yesterday, and Maria and Mark were coming back today, the last chance to see them for a while, unless the doctor allowed Mark in during her isolation. Sarah looked from a red heart-shaped balloon to a cuddly teddy bear and swallowed hard. It was so good to be home, with her friends to cheer her up and make her laugh.

And her mom—she was anxious but hopeful, nervous but determined—all at the same time. She had cried with happiness when they heard that Jamie was a compatible donor. The bone marrow transplant was risky, but it was also Sarah's best hope for recovery.

Sarah picked up the stuffed bear and held it close; she'd have to leave all these behind when she went into the isolation room, but her mom would take them home, save them for her to enjoy later, when the worst of her ordeal was behind her.

The phone rang, and she picked it up quickly.

"Sarah, how's it going? Is this a good time to come by?"

"Hi, Mark." Sarah smiled into the phone. "Perfect time. How was the trig test?"

"Rough, but I think I did okay," he told her. "I'll be by real soon; I have one more surprise for you."

He'd already brought her flowers and the teddy bear and several cards. "You don't have to," she murmured. "Seeing you is the best gift."

She heard him chuckle. "This is something a little different; you'll understand when I come."

After she hung up the phone, a knock sounded at the door. Sarah called, "Come in."

Maria put her head in the door. "Hi, Sarah. I saw your mom when I walked by the cafeteria; she said she'd be back up in a minute. She told me your grandmother's coming down tomorrow."

Sarah nodded. "Nana's lots better, and she wants to be here to help my mom so she doesn't wear herself out trying to stay at the hospital all the time."

"Your mom's a doll." Maria held up a brightly colored gift bag. "Look, I brought you something!"

"Oh, Maria, you didn't have to. The balloons yesterday were terrific," Sarah told her. "And the party was great."

"I wanted to," her best friend said. "Take a look."

Sarah pulled the tissue paper apart and reached into the bag. She felt silky fabric and pulled out a bright teal print scarf.

"For when your hair falls out," Maria pointed out. "So you can put on something pretty."

"Oh, Maria, thanks a bunch. It's gorgeous," Sarah told her, touching the soft fabric again. "This was really thoughtful; I'm still worried about what Mark will think when he sees me with a bald head."

"You know he's crazy about you, and it's not just because of your hair," Maria told her, sitting on the end of the bed.

"I know, I tell myself that, but still—" Sarah looked at Maria's thick dark curls and sighed.

Maria twisted a strand of her hair. "Easy for me to say, huh?"

Sarah giggled despite her anxiety. "Oh, well. It will grow back. Tell me what happened at school today."

"I'm taking notes for you in English class, and Annette is taping the government lectures. Mark will keep you up-to-date with trig, so you won't be

too far behind when you come back to school,"
Maria told her.

"I have the world's greatest friends—and family," Sarah said.

"You deserve to, after the bum deal you got with
the cancer and all." Maria frowned at the thought.

"My dad always said, you start where you are
and you go from there," Sarah said. "Whining
doesn't help much. Oh, is that Mark?"

Instead, it was her mom who opened the door.
She was smiling. "Hi, Maria. Sarah, you have another visitor."

"Must be the man," Maria said. "Hey, I've got
to run; we have practice at four. I'll call you tomorrow, amiga."

She waved and went out the door, but from the
hall, Sarah heard her friend squeal. What on earth
had Mark brought?

Her mom was grinning, too. "I'll just walk down
to the Coke machine," she said, winking at Sarah,
"and let you talk to Mark a few minutes."

"You are definitely the world's greatest mother,"
Sarah told her. "Tell him to come on in; I can't
imagine what his surprise is."

Her mom held the door, then slipped outside,
still smiling. But Mark was empty-handed. He was
wearing a new ball cap—surely that wasn't the
cause of Maria's giggles? And something about
him looked different, but—"

"Like my new haircut?"

Mark lifted the cap. Sarah gasped. He had

shaved his head! For a few seconds he looked totally strange, then—like her eyes adjusting to a change of light—he was simply Mark again, still good-looking with his straight nose and clear blue eyes, just a little more—exotic—than usual.

"Oh, Mark. Why?" But she knew why, and for a moment she had to blink hard.

"Just wanted to show you that a different hairstyle—or lack of one—isn't going to change how I feel about you, Sarah. I know you've been worrying about it, and when Maria told me she was out buying scarves yesterday, I got the idea. Like it? I think I could pass for a rock star, what do you think?"

So she laughed instead, and the tears disappeared. He came closer and squeezed her hand.

"How do you feel? Are you ready to start the whole ordeal?" His voice was more serious this time, but his eyes still twinkled.

Sarah had no trouble smiling back. "Absolutely. I'm ready to live."

Dear Diary

__Remember Me

by Cheryl Lanham
0-425-15194-8/$3.99

Leeanne never thought she'd love working at the hospice so much...or that it would be so hard. Her new friend Gabriel isn't like other boys. He is dying. But in his final days, he has one last lesson to teach her....

__Runaway

by Cheryl Zach
0-425-15047-X/$3.99

When Cassie becomes pregnant, Cassie's father sends her to a home for unwed mothers and forbids her from seeing her boyfriend again. Forced to choose between her family and the love of her life, Cassie begins to think of a drastic solution: running away.

__Family Secrets

by Cheryl Zach
0-425-15292-8/$3.99

Sarah has leukemia, and her only hope is a bone marrow transplant from a family member. But Sarah is adopted. In the fight to save her life, she must travel across the country looking for her birth mother...and a miracle.